BIG BOOK 2

Straight to gay

Kyle Rayne

SPIN THE BOTTLE

Straight to gay erotica

Kyle Rayne

Obviously, spin the bottle is a stupid and immature game played by teenagers... So why am I sitting cross-legged on a living room rug at thirty? After a game of beer pong, it just kinda happened.

Maybe everyone is too drunk to notice that there are more men than women in our circle. Everyone except for me... In any case, this party ended up being a sausage fest. I didn't come here to get laid, I just noticed things. I notice Brandon staring at me from across the circle as a drunk lady leans against my left side.

"It's my turn!" she shouts.

She spins the bottle haphazardly in the middle of the rug. The bottle points to someone I don't know. When he gets up, he drags her to the couch and puts her on his lap. There's no denying that it would be nice to kiss someone... I'll admit that I'm a little bi-curious (After a beer or two. Tomorrow I'll be a perfectly straight man).

As Brandon gazes directly at my eyes, he purrs, "It's my turn." The deep tone of his voice sends shivers down my spine. In a methodical manner, he places the sticky beer bottle on the rug then spins it slowly. He's trying to make it land on someone in particular. Who does Brandon want to kiss? Looking at the once large circle, it has significantly shrunk. My heart isn't really in it for kissing anyone here...

The bottle is pointed directly at me when Brandon sticks his foot out and purposely stops it. A female in the circle giggles, "It looks like Brandon and Nathon are kissing."

"What?" I gasped in surprise. Brandon didn't say anything.

My Adam's apple feels like a lump in my throat as I swallow hard. As Brandon stands up and grabs my hand to pull me up, I cannot find the words to say. Music is blaring loudly, and two women are already arguing over who gets to spin the bottle next. No one cares as he drags me down the hall to a bedroom.

Then he pulls me into a bedroom and locks the door behind us.

I finally got the courage to say, "We shouldn't be here. It doesn't feel right."

Seductively posing on the edge of the bed, he kicks off his Converse. I can appreciate this guy's husky, muscular physique, even though I'm straight.

As he props himself up on his elbows, he asks, "You don't want to kiss me because I'm a man or because this is someone else's bed?"

There's nothing I can do to stop my heart from pounding; it's the only thing I can hear. I don't even hear me say, "I don't want to kiss you in a stranger's bed. That feels wrong."

What is wrong with me? Why did I blurt that out? Do I actually want to kiss him?

He puts his hands under his head and lays flat on the duvet, posing very seductively.

"Luckily for you, this is my bed."

"Oh fuck!" I huffed out and Brandon chuckled. "I didn't know you lived here."

"I'm just a roommate. I moved in a week ago. I bought this bed brand new. I've haven't fucked anyone in it." He winked and added, "yet."

Oh my God… I wiped my sweaty palms on my jeans.

"Listen, Brandon. I'm straight."

He took a mint from his pocket and popped it in his mouth. His gesture suggests he wants to kiss someone.

He smiled wryly, "Then why are you standing in my bedroom with a boner?" He pointed to my pants. Embarrassed, I looked down.

"Fuck," I muttered and placed my hands over my dick. I knew it was pumping up but I hadn't realized it was poking out like that.

"Ok, so just a kiss. So, we can finish our stupid game."

He patted the bed, indicating I should lay down next to him.

"Just a kiss," he rasped, "Unless you want more, of course."

"Whatever."

I laid down on the bed... with a man... A big man that smelled nice and, "Oh f-fuck," I groaned when he sucked my bottom lip into his mouth. As we lay on our sides, I put my arm around his neck.

He slid his tongue into my mouth and it felt good... so good... The way he kissed me was so aggressive, yet soft at the same time. It was a perfect and intoxicating mixture. My dick was so hard I had to adjust it, Brandon chuckled into my mouth—it vibrated my chest and fuck, it exhilarated me.

I kept getting kissed, then he started touching me. It appealed to my curious side. I liked it more than I expected. He mapped my chest with his big, strong hand. Slowly, he traced his fingers through my hair that trailed under my navel and disappeared in my pants. Keeping my mouth busy, he stuck one finger into my jeans and boxers and left it there.

I pulled away from the kiss. "What the fuck?"

He cocked an eyebrow at me. "Fuck indeed."

I sat up. "Okay, we kissed. Are you happy now?"

"I am happy. You're a good kisser. Don't you find yourself wanting…. more?"

I did… I did want more… I wanted it… If only I could break through the barrier holding me back. After getting out of bed, I headed for his door.

"If you change your mind, you know where to find me," Brandon said.

I stopped and faced the door. "If you and I—" I didn't have the courage to say the word. "What does that make me?" I asked.

"If we have sex, it doesn't make you anything. It just means we are two consenting adults that are enjoying each other's company."

Dammit, there's a good chance I'm a closet gay. There's only one way to find out. I turned around to face Brandon. In front of him, I stuck my hand in my pants and shamelessly adjusted my raging boner.

"Need help with that?" he taunted while pointing to my erection. "If you're leaving, you can go now so I can rub one out." Looking between his legs, he had a bulge like mine.

"Maybe I can help you with your boner? And you can help me with mine?" I couldn't believe I just said that! What was wrong with me?

I watched him with rapt attention as he peeled off his shirt. "Come back to bed. More kisses, please."

I sat down on the edge of his bed. "Shoes off," Brandon said while eyeing my shoes, "and your shirt."

"Fuck, ok."

We were kissing ravenously the next thing I knew. Our flat chests rubbing together felt amazing as he rolled me on my back. It was so unexpected how much different it was to make out with a guy. It was different in a good way.

Kissing a man was erotic and exhilarating. I felt intoxicated like I was on a drug. I dug my hips into his and grabbed a handful of his short curls. Through our pants, our dicks rubbed against each other.

I pulled away from our kiss. "My zipper is hurting my balls."

"Shall we take our pants off then?" Right next to my dick, he rubbed my thighs

"Yes, yes, we should," I rasped. In the blink of an eye our pants were gone.

The only thing we wore was our boxers. We were almost naked.

And f-fuck… I wanted to be completely naked. I wanted my dick and balls pressed against his. The thought made my dick drip precum—I had a wet spot in front of my boxers.

Brandon hadn't suggested getting naked. I figured out what he was doing—he was letting me take the lead. Wherever this went was up to me. I wanted this… badly. The next time his dick pressed against mine with our boxer barrier, I couldn't stop the moan that radiated from my belly.

Brandon didn't suggest getting naked. It made sense to me that he was letting me take the lead. I was entirely in control. I got to decide where this ended up. I wanted this… really bad. I couldn't stop moaning as his dick pressed against mine through our boxers.

"Oh fuck, Brandon," I rasped, "Your dick is so thick. I can feel it."

"Just say the words and I'll take my boxers off."

"Ditch the drawers," I rasped. My voice sounded like I'd been eating gravel. "And I'll take mine off."

As Brandon took off his boxers, he gave me a show. Fuck, he had a nice body. His muscles were chiseled. He had firm, shapely pecs. He had obliques for days, and I liked them. My eyes were drawn to his dick by the V carved into his hips. Compared to him, I was an average guy.

When he pulled his boxers down slowly, I watched his dick pop out, and I groaned when I saw his balls. It was tempting to reach out and touch them, but I didn't. His sac looked red, heavy and tight. Both of us needed to cum.

Playfully, he pushed me on my back.

"I want to see your dick," he pleaded.

My attention was so captivated by the sight of his dick that I forgot to take off my boxers.

"Fuck, alright. I'll take my boxers off"

"Are you nervous?" he cautiously asked.

"I... I guess I am."

He caressed my chest. "Relax, I won't bite. Not unless you want me to," he said with a wink.

"Ok then," I rasped and hastily pulled my boxers off. I wasn't nearly as graceful as Brandon, but hey, I got the job done.

My dick was standing ramrod straight. He put his hands on my thighs. "Can I touch you?" he politely asked.

"Yes, you can touch me. Please touch me." Until now, I hadn't realized how much I wanted it.

My first thought was that he would wrap his fist around my shaft. Instead, he licked my dripping tip. On the underside of my crown, he flicked his tongue around the sensitive V.

"Oh God," he rasped, "you taste so good."

"Thanks," I squeaked out.

I felt my head being sucked into his mouth. As he looked at me with his eyes half open and lidded with lust, he said coyly, "I bet you've never had your dick sucked like this."

"No, I haven't."

After he swallowed my dick entirely, I rasped, "Oh, my fucking, fuck." It was like my head was bouncing off his throat. Instead of gagging, he moaned on my shaft. While sucking me, he stroked me.

As his mouth glided up and down my dick, I was enchanted. This is the most fucking sexy thing I've ever seen. Yeah, I've had my dick sucked before, but never with such enthusiasm. It's like a chore for some women I've slept with. The only reason they did it was because I begged them. Brandon was enjoying himself, though, so it was even better. This was a mind-blowing blow job. When he moaned on my shaft, it only amplified the intensity! My hips bucked as I gripped the bedsheets.

"H-holy fuck!" I cried out. "I'm so close to coming. I'm right on the edge." My mind was racing because I wasn't sure whether it was okay to blow my load into his mouth, or not.

His head lifted and he spat out my cock. "Do you want to cum in my hand, mouth or my ass?"

"Oh shit," I rasped, "I get to choose?"

He let out a sultry chuckle. "Yes, of course."

"Geezus," I huffed, "That's a hard choice."

"This doesn't have to be a onetime thing. So, don't feel like you'll only get one chance to get what you want," Brandon explained.

One minute I was playing spin the bottle, and the next, I had a boyfriend who loved to deep throat and would let me cum in his ass. Hooray for me!

"What do you prefer?" I asked.

"You can cum anywhere you'd like, but I'm in the mood for you to fuck my ass."

"Fuck yeah!" I huffed out like a horny teenager.

Brandon grabbed a bottle of lube from his nightstand and squirted some in his palm. He rubbed it up and down my shaft with his strong hand.

"Go slow because you didn't prep me." He must have noticed my perplexed expression when he added, "That means to stretch me out with a toy or fingers first."

"Do I need to do that?"

"I'll be fine as long as you don't rail me initially."

"I understand."

His legs were spread obscenely wide as he lay flat on his back. It was sexy as hell. My eyes were completely captivated by his sexy naked body, sprawled out on the sheets. My first move was to get between his knees. In order to spread him wider, I put my elbows under the crooks of his knees. My dick glided down his hair-covered crack. There was something fucking sexy about his body hair. It was so different from a woman's body. I don't see anything wrong with that if you like it...

It became clear to me as I pressed my dick into his tight ring of muscle that it was a one-way street for me. It would be impossible for me to go back to fucking women. You know what's weird? I didn't like sleeping with any of the women. I just didn't know there was an alternative.

Slowly, I sank my dick into Brandon's ass. I could feel his fingers digging into my thighs and he was biting his bottom lip. My fear made me stop pushing, I didn't want to hurt him.

"Fuck, your dick feels so good. Don't stop, push it in all the way," he rasped with his eyebrows scrunched.

"Okay... fuck," I rasped and sank my dick in balls deep. I was deep... so deep in his channel. He was so tight and so warm.

"That's it, you're all the way in," he purred, "you can fuck me now."

That was an offer I couldn't refuse.

At first, I thrust my dick in and out slowly. It was a moment I wanted to savor forever. It was my first time having gay sex... I never wanted it to end. I knew I would cum soon as I watched my dick slide in and out of his pink star-shaped flesh.

Brandon gripped my hips tightly and thrust his hips to meet mine. With more leverage, he pushed himself in deeper, and I didn't know that was possible.

I repeatedly slammed my dick in his ass. It wasn't just my dick that felt pleasure. My entire body felt good. He stroked his dick lazily while his hole quivered around my shaft.

Those sensations... I knew I'd cum soon when my nuts were tight to my body. As a matter of fact, I was going to cum right now. I felt my load shoot out of my dick, into his ass. As I tilted my head back, I roared, "Oh fuck Brandon! I'm coming so hard!"

"Me too! I'm... coming so hard!" he screamed.

In a steady flow, Brandon's white cream poured from his slit as he squeezed his head. Damn, I bet that felt good.

Brandon

Getting laid was not what I expected from a game of spin the bottle. For a long time, I've had a boyish crush on Nate. And now he's breathless, sticky, and collapsed on top of me in my bed.

We had sticky chests from my cum, and it wasn't as warm as it was moments ago, but I kissed him on the neck anyway. I wasn't done with Nate yet. There was still so much to explore sexually. I didn't know if he was into ass-play. I'd love to fuck his ass, but only if he wants me to.

"Come on, let's go clean up. Lucky for you, I have a large walk-in shower."

"Shit, okay," he muttered. I thought it was cute when he nervously ran his fingers through his hair.

He seemed a little cagey.

"Don't freak out. Are you okay?" I knew this was his first-time having sex with a man. It could be a bit much for first-timers. This is especially true for closet cases that have been in denial for a long time.

"I'm fine, let's go shower."

We entered my shower, which is conveniently located next to my bedroom. With my hand lathered in soap, I washed out my ass cheeks. I always liked the feeling of cum leaking out of my ass. Why does it feel so good? I don't know... It just does.

I handed Nate my soap. As he washed his hair with my shampoo, he was so quiet.

"Something on your mind?" I asked. I watched the soap suds drip from his hair, down his chest and drip off his balls. So sexy...

"You seemed to like it in the ass."

I couldn't help but to laugh. "Well, yes of course. I like it because it feels good." I sensed a question in his words. "You've never touched yourself back there?" I asked.

"Never," he chuckled. I always wondered how someone never played with their own body parts, but whatever.

"You should try it." I couldn't hide my flirtatious smile. "The only way to know if you'll like something new is to try it."

"Right now?" he choked out. That's not what I meant, but it was an excellent suggestion!

"Yes, of course. Try it right now." As the shower water sprayed across us, I watched him in anticipation.

"Do it, please. I want to watch you touch yourself for the first time," I thought to myself.

I grabbed his hand and squirted some conditioner on his fingers.

"Now you're all lubed up. No harm in just one touch, if you don't like it, just move your hand." He gazed at me intensely, like he was considering it. "You're in control. Unless... You want me to do it for you?" Please say yes. I want to be the first man to touch him back there... On his virgin ass.

He turned around and put his hands on the shower wall and spread his legs. My dick was already getting hard before he spoke.

"Do it for me. You have more experience doing this stuff."

"Oh God yes." I squirt conditioner on my finger. I caressed his ass cheek, relishing the moment. Then I slipped my finger into his crack and found what I was looking for.

"Wow, that feels good and you haven't even touched my hole yet."

"Just you wait. I'll make you feel so good."

I circled his hole and he moaned—that's a good sign.

"Mmmpffff," he rasped.

I just circled his hole to tease him—to test the waters.

"Shall I continue?" I asked.

"Yes, but let's shut off this water and go back to bed. I'm turning into a raisin here."

"Good idea."

The hot water tank was probably empty now because of us. I would never turn down a chance to take a man back to my bed. A chance to make him feel good and make him mine.

"Get on all fours for me," I told Nate.

"Ok." He did exactly that, and buried his face in my pillow. There were some stray water droplets on his ass and balls—I don't know why that was so sexy... but it was.

I leaned forward and sniffed him, and surprisingly Nate didn't say anything. He smelt fresh and clean—perfect for licking. I felt like a dog for doing that, but I wanted to know what his scent was like. I licked him across his hole and he quivered.

"Damn that feels good," Nate rasped.

"Mmm," I moaned while licking him. That's all I needed to hear. He said what I was doing to him was making him feel good. I pushed my tongue into his hole, trying to move past the barrier.

"Oh f-fuck!" he cried, "That's amazing!"

Suddenly, my dick was hard again after thrusting my tongue into his ass. He might let me put my dick inside of him if I was lucky. I have never been 'the lucky guy.' I have never won anything. The moment he said, "Please fuck me," I felt like I had won the lottery.

"Of course." I grabbed my lube from my nightstand. "I stretched you a little with my tongue. Shall I use my fingers first?"

"No. I just want you," he rasped. "I want your dick inside of me."

I squirt lube on my shaft. "It might sting at first, but it will stop."

"I'll be fine. I'm a tough guy."

Oh fuck... he wanted this just as bad as me.

I slid between his legs on my sheets. I grabbed my dick and pressed it at his opening... That virgin ass. He'd have one last chance to back out.

"Are you sure you want this?"

"Very sure," he replied in a deep, needy voice. "I want you to fuck me." I wouldn't deny him anything.

I pushed my dick slowly into his tight ring of muscle. He was so tight and I loved feeling his hole quiver around my shaft.

Nate was moaning and mumbling. "Oh… Oh…"

I stopped thrusting in his ass. "Are you ok?"

"Oh baby," he rasped, "I'm more than okay. I don't think I've ever felt so good. Please don't stop fucking me."

"Whatever you want."

I started thrusting into him again. I loved watching my shaft glide in and out his flesh.

"Fuck me harder," he added.

"Alright." I grasped his hips and slammed into him as hard and fast as I could. "Oh, that ass feels so fucking good." My heart was hammering in my chest!

"That dick… that dick feels so good… Fucking. My. Ass." He moaned each word between my thrusts.

I was about to cum again, so quickly. I'm usually not like that. Fucking back-to-back was usually hard. But here I was, trying not to cum, fucking his ass. In an attempt to hold it in, I squeezed my groin muscles. In fact, I grabbed my dick at the base. Nothing I read online to prolong my orgasm would work. Not when I was railing Nate's virgin ass. Not to mention a straight man's ass.

There was only one problem: I knew he wasn't straight. Years ago, I was like him...

I felt my nuts hugging up tight to my body. I reached around and grabbed Nate's dick and jerked it for him as I came. His dick was swollen—he needed to cum.

I jerked his dick, because I was coming in his ass and I wanted to drag him along for the ride.

"Come for me baby!" I rasped. I stroked his shaft the way I liked to touch mine. I jerked him in a figure-eight pattern.

"H-holy fuck!" he moaned and his hole started quivering around my shaft. He was coming, along with me.

I spurt rope after rope of cum deep into his ass. Nate looked back at me with his cheeks flushed red. "There's probably a wet spot on your brand-new mattress. I'm so sorry."

I kissed him on the back. "Don't be sorry. That's perfect! Thanks for helping me break in my new bed."

Nate awkwardly chuckled. "Yeah, of course. Anytime."

I pulled my flaccid dick out of his pink hole, my white cream gushed out too. It was a beautiful sight.

"Spend the night," I told Nate. "Only if you feel comfortable."

He ran his hands through his hair. "Yeah, sure."

I pulled him into my chest and snuggled into my blanket. I wasn't sure if he'd cuddle with me, but he did. I fell asleep with his head tucked into my chest.

The next morning, I woke up and felt a hard dick pressed into my thigh.

"Damn morning wood," Nate rasped.

"Let me suck you off." I would get him off as many times as I could before he left.

"Let's suck each other's dicks. I want to taste you," Nate rasped. That's the magic words every gay man wants to hear from a guy who's experimenting for the first time. I couldn't wait to find out if he'd swallow.

"Let's lay on our sides, it's comfortable to sixty-nine like that."

As we lay on our sides, I sucked him into my mouth. He grabbed my shaft lightly with his teeth, then he slurped my head into his mouth. He was freaky and I liked it...

It was so warm and so wet in his mouth... Oh fuck...

He was moaning on my shaft already, so I knew he liked it. I wasn't going to last this long, so I spit his dick out and said, "I'm going to cum!" I thought he would spit me out, but he sucked me harder and harder. He wanted me to cum in his mouth.

While I was shooting my load into his mouth, he was coming into mine. We sucked each other dry. Each of us sucked the life out of the other.

Nate was breathless. "I need to say something."

"Yes?" I wasn't sure where he was going with this, but I had a feeling.

He held his breath and blew it out. "I'm gay."

I kissed him on the forehead. "I know sweetheart."

The end

TOPPED

Straight to gay erotica

Kyle Rayne

My first day at the coffee shop seems like it was yesterday. I started working here almost a year ago. I'm a barista, and while it's not the most glamorous job in the world, it pays the bills and I get free coffee. Free coffee is the best thing in the world.

Almost every day, there are patrons who come in with their laptops and do whatever they do. Even though it's not my business, I've always wondered what customers are doing.

To get to the bathroom, I had to walk behind the customer's tables, and today, I saw one of our regulars' computer screen. My eye only caught it for a half-second. I'm pretty sure he was writing something dirty. I think he writes erotica! It was definitely a sexy piece of writing.

I laughed as I walked out of the bathroom and saw that he had switched seats. From this angle, I can't see his computer screen. It's rude to look over someone's shoulder, but I wanted to see what he was writing.

I began making coffee and tea once I got behind the counter again. The man writing erotica walked up to the register. When he was eyeing me at the counter, I almost spilled hot coffee all over myself. He already paid for his coffee... What else did he want?

"Can I help you?" I had no idea who he was despite seeing him several times a week. I didn't know his name.

"I'll take a breakfast sandwich." He then told me what else he wanted. He sat at his laptop while I prepared his food. Silly me… Of course he didn't get up to flirt with me. Or did he?

I brought his food over to him and asked, "So, what do you do on that computer of yours?" I'm probably going to get fired. I'll lose my job because he'll complain to my manager. Although he's cute, I'm not sure he's worth it.

"I'm an author. I'm writing a book," he rasped.

Fuck, he knows I saw his screen earlier. His smoldering gaze tells me either he's pissed or annoyed. It might be both. I thought he wrote gay erotica, but I could be totally wrong. Maybe it was just my desperate, sex-starved imagination.

"That's cool," I said as I turned to leave.

"Wait!" he shouted. "Did you see my screen?"

My Adam's apple bobbed as I swallowed nervously. "Nope. Why would you say that?"

Taking a bite of his sandwich, he said, "Because you're blushing. Most people don't appreciate that type of literature during their workday."

"I guess I'm busted then," I laughed nervously, "It wasn't my intention to look. It was an accident. I'm really sorry."

"It's fine," he said as he sipped his coffee.

"Can I read your stories sometime?" I curiously asked. There was definitely something sexy about him… I couldn't deny that I felt curious.

"Sure." He reached into his laptop case for a pen and notepad. "Here's my phone number."

Taking the paper, I slipped it into my pocket. That's it, I'm getting fired. We aren't supposed to fraternize with our customers. I thought he'd just tell me where to find his book. It's probably online, but I have to call him to find out.   I'll have to get in touch with him to see what he writes. I'll admit that I'm curious. I'm also curious about sleeping with men. It's something I've never done before, but I really want to.

After my shift, I texted him because that's how most people communicate. On the tiny piece of paper, he wrote his name: *Keith.*

"Hey Keith, it's Jake from the coffee shop," I texted.

"Hi! I didn't think I'd ever hear from you LOL."

"Why?"

"Because I'm gay and single," Keith texted.

Oh my god... What do I say now? I couldn't think of anything to text in response, so I put my phone in my pocket. This appeals to my curious side though. After shoving my phone in my pocket for two seconds, it vibrated two seconds later.

"What are you doing?" Keith texted.

"Nothing."

"Come over to my house. I'll show you my books."

Oh fuck... What should I do? If I said I didn't want to go over to his house, I'd be lying to myself...

I knocked on the door of his apartment. When he answered the door, he was almost naked. The only thing he wore was a pair of basketball shorts. I could clearly see his dick-print through the thin fabric.

"Hey Jake. Come on in," he purred.

I had one last chance to back out. Either I could go into a gay man's house or I could go home. I walked into his apartment before I could stop myself. It smelled like coffee brewing.

"Didn't you have coffee at the cafe?" I awkwardly asked.

"Yes, but coffee is fuel for my brain to write my books."

"Fair enough. Coffee is life."

I knew right then and there he would fuck me if I didn't leave when he looked at me seductively in the eyes.

My gaze wandered down his nearly-naked body. He had a nicely-shaped body. His arms, chest, and thighs were muscular. However, the rest of his body was lean. Under his navel, there was a trail of hair that disappeared into the waistband of his shorts. I was transfixed by the trail of hair and where it led.

He cocked an eyebrow and asked, "Like what you see?"

I felt so embarrassed! I was caught staring and checking him out! There was no point in lying since I was busted.

"Yes. Yes, I do."

"Good boy," he purred. His deep, seductive voice sent shivers down my spine. I was so screwed—literally.

I froze when he cupped my chin. "Tell me Jake. Do you top or bottom?"

What were we talking about? This was some lingo unfamiliar to me.

"What?" I choked out.

He pulled his hand back and crossed his arms.

"For some reason, I took you to be a power-bottom," he said matter-of-factly.

He was definitely speaking English, but I felt like he was speaking in a dialect I didn't understand.

"Umm…" I nervously ran my fingers through my hair. "I don't know what you are talking about." I felt my face flush in embarrassment, especially when his jaw gaped open in shock.

"You… You've never had sex with a man?"

"Nope," I squeaked out. I don't think I've ever seen such a shocked expression on someone's face.

He stepped closer to me, and he smelt nice. "But you came over anyway? Why?"

"I'm curious. I've never tried it, but it doesn't mean I don't want to."

I felt like such a stupidass. He was probably expecting someone who was experienced. Someone who could suck his dick and be a 'power-bottom,' whatever that was. "Maybe I should go," I added.

"You don't have to go." He wrapped his arms around my neck. "Can I kiss you?"

My heart was hammering in my chest. "Yes."

He closed his eyes and pressed his mouth against mine. I liked how he tasted like mouthwash and coffee—it was a good combination. He slipped his tongue into my mouth. Fuck... kissing him felt good.

I could feel his dick through his flimsy shorts as he pressed our bodies together. It was semi-erect, not fully hard. I felt him grasp the nape of my neck and moan into my mouth. While kissing me, he swayed his head from side to side. He was one hell of a kisser!

The way he was moaning and touching me meant one thing. This man wanted sex from me! Was I going to give it to him? Oh yes... yes I was.

He pulled away from me, breathless and eyes lidded heavily with lust.

"We would be more comfortable in my bed."

"Yes we would. Let's go."

I was definitely going to let him take me to his bed. Something about him was so intoxicating to me that I felt like putty in his hands.

It didn't take Keith long to get comfortable on his bed. Standing at the end of his bed, I looked at him.

"Well," he purred, "Aren't you going to join me?"

I sat down on the foot of his bed. "Yes I am."

"Don't you want to get more comfortable?" he asked.

"Yes."

I wore jeans and a hoodie. It was my last chance to back out, but I really wanted this! With the exception of my boxers, I stripped off all my clothes. He looked so fucking sexy sprawled out on his bed. Astonished at his body, I scooted up to him.

"So, what is a power-bottom? Or, top?" I shyly asked.

A huge smile spread across his face as he kissed my neck. "I'm going to have so much fun dragging you out of the closet," he said, dragging his tongue across my nipple. He sucked my pebbled nipple into his mouth.

"Oh fuck that feels good, but you didn't answer my question."

A devious expression appeared on his face as he looked at me. "You are going to love being topped, which means I'm on top. You'll be on the bottom."

"Oh!" It all suddenly made sense. Duh!

That meant.... Oh my God... I wanted it...

Then he kissed my body to distract me from asking anymore questions. My dick was definitely trickling up with blood as he kissed his way down my stomach. Keith kissed my stomach —it was wet and messy. It was making me want his mouth elsewhere... I really wanted it.

He kissed my stomach at the edge of my boxers. It was obvious my dick was tenting them! I felt Keith stick a finger in my waistband, on my hips.

Deeply, he rasped, "If you want me to suck your dick, just say the words."

How could I refuse an offer like that?

As I pulled my boxers down, I said, "I want you to suck my dick." My cock stood ramrod straight, and I wondered what Keith was thinking. He was a complete stranger to me. Having sex with a stranger is something I've never done before...

"Your dick looks delicious and suckable," he rasped.

He sucked me into his mouth just as I was about to thank him. He had a wet mouth... so wet and warm. And he sucked me so *hard*. There was nothing better than the slurping sound of his mouth gliding up and down my dick.

I grabbed a handful of the short hair on his head and moaned, "Oh my fucking God." My dick bounced off his throat as I pushed my hips up. Another man sucking my dick was the sexiest thing I've ever seen. Of course, I've thought about it (a man sucking me off), but the feeling of him sucking me is so sexy.

It was only natural for me to return the favor.

"I want to suck your dick," I mumbled.

Wild-eyed, he looked up at me. "Let's sixty-nine."

"I'm guessing I'm on the bottom?"

"Yes, of course."

Keith flipped around and shoved his ass in my face—it was a nice ass. After that, he straddled my face. His dick was pointed towards my mouth as he grabbed the base. In order to swallow him, I lifted my head.

His hips pushed forward as he rasped, "Oh fuck."

My mouth slid up and down his shaft. It didn't take me long to get the hang of sucking dick. His dick was leaking, my mouth was filled with droplets of precum. Fuck, he tasted delicious, salty and tangy.

"Mmm," I moaned onto his shaft as he sucked me in.

It felt good sucking each other's dicks. It's better than good. My groin burned with pleasure I couldn't even begin to describe. Especially when he wrapped his hand around my shaft, and stroked me and sucked me at the same time. I was going to cum soon.

I felt a finger slide into my crack and I was shocked. My hips bucked! He spit my dick out.

"Should I not touch you back there?"

"Touch me. It felt good. I was just surprised."

I was breathless after sucking dick and I wanted more. My mouth slurped as I swallowed him. When I felt a finger circle my hole, I moaned, so Keith would know I wanted more! I didn't want to say anything. I wanted to keep sucking him off. To keep his dick in my mouth, I grabbed his wrist and pushed his finger into my hole. I felt my dick slip out of his mouth and he spit on my hole. Why was that so hot? Slowly, he inserted a finger into my hole.

I had to spit his dick out this time.

"Fuck that feels good," I rasped.

"Glad you like it. I want to make you feel so good."

While he kept pumping his finger in and out of my ass, my dick bucked, wanting to be stroked.

Getting finger-fucked felt good, but I wanted more… so much more. The only thing I wanted was for him to fuck me. It never occurred to me that penetration would feel so damn good.

"Keith, will you fuck me?" I rasped.

Through his lashes, he peeked coyly at me as he licked my shaft. "I knew you'd enjoy this. Yes, I will fuck you. You're gonna be my sexy, little power-bottom."

A huff escaped my lips, "Oh." I think I understand the concept now. "You can call me whatever you want. As long as you fuck me."

I don't think I've ever seen anyone smile like that, when he said, "Okay. Lay down flat on your back for me and spread your legs."

As instructed, I spread my legs wide.

Keith

Jake, the barista, was going to let me fuck him. As he lay naked in my bed, I almost couldn't believe my eyes. While sitting at my laptop, I have seen him countless times. The fact that he was always busy made it easy for me to check him out. It was cute how oblivious he was.

Now he's in the flesh, on my bed, ready for me to fuck him.

I rolled a condom down my shaft and greased it for extra measure. I wanted it to be well-lubricated for him. Jake's eyes were lidded heavy with lust as I got between his legs. I spread him out wider with my knees.

"I'm going to put your legs on my shoulders," I told Jake.

"Shit, okay," he rasped while slowly jerking his dick.

I put his legs on my shoulders and found what I was looking for—his pink star-shaped quivering hole. I grabbed my lube and squirted some on his hole. I really didn't want to hurt him.

Jake giggled, "That was really cold!"

"Sorry about that, I'll warm up that ass lickety-split." I pushed my head into his opening and it was tight… too tight.

"Take a deep breath." Jake sucked in a mouthful of air. "Breathe in through your nose, and out through your mouth. Your channel will open up for me." That's probably not a well-known bit of advice, but it really works!

He sucked in a breath through his nose, and when he exhaled out of his mouth, I was able to slide right into him.

"Of fuck, you feel so good" I moaned. He was tight and warm, but not too tight this time. "Are you ok?" I added. His eyebrows were scrunched and his cheeks flushed red. It could either mean he was in pain, or experiencing pleasure. Or a combination of both.

"Oh, I'm good, so good. Please fuck me," he rasped.

Somehow, I knew he would want to bottom. Sometimes I like it as well. It entirely depends on my mood. I'm in the mood to fuck right now. So, top it is.

Initially, I slid my dick in and out slowly. And fuck, it felt so good sliding balls deep.

"Mmm," I groaned in response. I had no words as I railed his tight ring of muscle, stretched beautifully around my girth.

The next thing I knew, he was digging his blunt fingernails into my back and moaning, "Oh fuck, this feels so fucking good!" He was thrusting his hips to meet mine. This was such a thrill because I was the first person who got to fuck his ass. I was the guy who showed him how good penetration feels.

I wrapped my fist around his girth and stroked him as I fucked him. I timed my stroking with the thrusts of my hips.

"Oh fucking baby," he moaned. I didn't even know I had him so close, but he was shooting his load all over his stomach and chest. His eyes were shut tight and he was moaning and gripping my ass-cheeks.

"Oh fuck... oh fuck... I'm coming so hard!" he rasped. His hole was quivering around my dick and it truly milked my shaft. From my balls through my shaft, pleasure burned through me as my load pumped out, filling up the condom.

"Oh f-fuck," I moaned, "I'm coming!"

Spurt after spurt drained from my balls until I was completely spent. I collapsed on top of him. I kissed his neck, then slid my dick out of his hole. I could tell by the look in his eyes, he might have a freak-out moment.

"Are you ok?" I asked.

He raked his hands through his hair and down his face. "Yeah, I'm fine. But I need to go."

I knew his type. He's not necessarily the 'hit-and-run' type of guy. He just needed some personal space to process what he just did.

A few days went by and I didn't hear from Jake. He didn't answer my texts or calls. I hadn't known if what we did was a one-time thing or not. Of course I wanted him in my bed again, but not if he wasn't interested. I hoped he didn't regret what we did...

I've been going to the coffee shop long enough to know that Jake is off Thursdays. I ordered my usual and set up my laptop, connecting to the WIFI. As usual, I'm completely zoned out writing my current erotica book. I don't even look away from my computer screen until I have to piss.

It's time for me to go to the bathroom. In this particular coffee establishment, there is only one bathroom stall. There is a huge bathroom inside, but it is set up for a single person. There is only a toilet, urinal, and hand sink.

Naturally, I'm shocked when someone follows me in. My brain isn't able to process what happened because it happened so fast. When I turned around, it was Jake.

Having drank coffee all day, I go about my business.

"Ghost on me for days and stalk me in the bathroom?" I cautiously asked.

"I'm sorry, really I am."

Once finished, I washed my hands and looked back at him in the mirror. "How sorry are you?"

"Really sorry."

I turned to face him. "We don't have to have sex again, Jake."

His face turned beet-red. "But I want to have sex with you again."

"Okay, well, call me later." I went to open the bathroom door and he side-stepped me.

"Now," he huffed, "Can we have sex right now?"

I couldn't stop the deep laugh that escaped me. "Don't you have to work?"

"I don't need to clock in for ten more minutes."

Was I going to fuck Jake in the bathroom at his workplace? Oh fuck yes... yes I was.

He kissed me and pushed me into the wall and was frantically undoing my button and zipper. My cock sprang free and he dropped to his knees, on the dirty bathroom floor.

"What about your uniform pants?" I asked in amusement as he sucked my dick into his mouth, but he spit it out.

"I have spares in the car. Used to spill coffee on myself a lot." Then he slurped me back into his mouth.

He cupped my sac and his wet lips glided up and down my shaft. I ran my fingers through his short hair and moaned.

"God, I want to fuck you. Right here and right now."

This was so dirty, but I wanted it...

My dick popped out of his mouth and he stood up and started unbuckling his belt.

"Jake," I laughed, "I don't have a condom." I didn't know him that well, so I wasn't going swimming without a raincoat.

He pulled a rubber out of his pocket. "Here."

Now, I was really laughing. "Came prepared?"

"I was just hopeful."

Jake turned around and braced his hands against the wall. With one hand, he pulled his shirt up in the back. His pants and boxers were around his ankles, so he could only spread his legs so wide. I palmed the globes of his ass and saw where I wanted to bury my cock. Then I cupped his sac, it was heavy, yet tight.

I spread his cheeks wide and saw his puckering, pink hole. "I'm gonna fuck that ass," I muttered.

"Please, please fuck me," he begged.

"Oh yes baby."

I pushed my crown into his opening and slid balls deep quicker this time. I slid in and out of his hole and fuck... it felt amazing. With each thrust, I slid home, balls deep.

We would run out of time soon. He had to clock in soon and I was worried someone would knock on the door. Other dudes gotta piss... I needed to make this quickie... quick!

This time I thrust in and out of him quickly. The sound of our bodies slamming together was obscenely loud, echoing in the small space. Anyone standing outside the door could probably hear it.

I loved watching my shaft engulfed in his flesh. And it felt so fucking good. He was so tight. But not too tight this time, the pressure was perfect. When his ass was too tight, it was almost painful for me. If I had to guess, I'd say he might have found something to masturbate with.

"Stretching yourself?" I moaned.

"Y-yes," Jake rasped.

"Bought yourself a toy?" I teased.

"Yes."

Ha, I knew it.

"It's not as good as my dick though?"

"No," he moaned. "It's so much better when you fuck me."

I agreed but didn't care to comment. I was busy fucking his amazing ass. My nuts were hugged up tight to my body and tingling. I was going to cum. But I wanted Jake to get off before he had to work. I would be the man who would turn him into a boneless, fucked-out mess in the bathroom.

"Stroke your dick," I rasped.

I couldn't do it for him. My hands were gripping his cheeks, holding them open. And I was about to cum, although I was trying to hold out. For just a minute longer. Just a moment... So Jake could get off first. I wanted him to blow his load all over the floor. Isn't that sick, perverted and a little twisted? I didn't think so. I already knew I was a perv. But this was my first time fucking in a bathroom that wasn't mine.

Here I was, fucking a nearly-stranger in a public bathroom. It was a dirty act in itself, yet so sexy in a way I couldn't explain.

I watched his arm frantically moving up and down as he stroked himself. He moved his hand away, and licked it, then spit on it before wrapping it around his shaft again. That dirty, yet sexy act pushed me over the edge. I was coming so hard.

"Oh fuck Jake!" I rasped out, louder than I intended.

"I'm... I'm coming," he moaned. I heard the wet sounds of his cum dripping on the tile floor.

I pumped up the condom with my load, and fuck, it was a big one. I was breathless and boneless. I wished we were on my bed in my apartment. I'd probably fall right asleep.

"Can you call in sick?" I asked. "You can come back to my apartment and chill." I was full of after-sex endorphins and actually, I wanted to cuddle and kiss for hours! Don't make fun of me!

I took off the rubber and tossed it in the trash.

"I can't. My boss already knows I'm here."

I cupped his chin and kissed his cheek.

"Come over when you are done working. You know where I live."

Jake pulled up his pants and buttoned them. He blushed and said. "Yeah, I'll swing by later."

"Promise you won't ghost on me this time?"

"I promise."

"Come here," I told Jake. "You look like a fucked-out mess."

I ran my hands down his shirt in an attempt to smooth out the wrinkles. I then wet a hand to try to flatten his hair.

"There, I think you look presentable enough. Hopefully your boss won't notice."

"Hopefully." He opened the bathroom door. "You still didn't show me your books."

"I will next time. But you're going to fuck me first. I'm in the mood to bottom."

"Sounds good."

The end

The end

WET

Straight to gay

Kyle Rayne

I t's my problem that I haven't been laid in over six months. Here's what I mean. It's never easy to break up, and this was especially true with my last partner. I shouldn't have stayed with him for as long as I did, but it's over, so I'm moving on. We've been broken up for six months. The past six months I ate cookies and pizza didn't do much for my health.

Now, I've been working out and trying to get healthier. There's no need for me to be ripped. I just wanna firm up, tighten up my ass, buff up my pecs and biceps. Self-care is important to me.

So, here I am at the gym, minding my own business on the treadmill. There are always tons of guys at the gym where I work out. While I'm not here to flirt and make anyone uncomfortable, I do let my eyes wander.

Hot guys flexing their biceps. Hot guys bending over with kettle-bells. Oh God, the things I would do to that ass... if only they would let me.

On my left, a voice purred, "Hello."

"Hi," I replied.

"It's always so busy this time of day."

I looked over and saw he was another good-looking guy. In general, I wasn't drawn to anything in particular. Usually, I was attracted to something else than a particular type of guy. For instance, a personality. My ex-partner was a bad boy, but not in a sexy way. He was a fucking prick…

"Yeah, it's hard to find machines that are open when it's busy. So, I just walk until the crowd thins out."

I was trying to cover my tracks. If he knew I was checking guys out… What would he think? I guess I didn't care anyway.

"There's a lot of fresh meat out there, isn't there?" he said with a wry smile slathered on his face and winked.

I choked out, "Excuse me?"

He nonchalantly shrugged. "Oh, so you weren't checking anyone out?"

He just flat out called me out. Guess there was no point in lying. "Yes, I suppose I was."

My face flushed red with embarrassment and I proceeded to fiddle with my phone instead of talking to this annoying stranger.

While mindlessly scrolling through Twitter on the treadmill, my phone sat on the electronic device shelf. A hand reached over and grabbed my phone. It was that annoying stranger.

"Hey dude, what the fuck?"

He flicked a dismissive hand. "Calm down. I'm giving you my

phone number. If you want to... You know. Give me a call." He hopped off the treadmill and he was gone.

As he walked towards the locker room, I took a good look at him. He has dark hair and a lot of ink on his left arm. He had a good-looking, round, pert ass that looked ripe for fucking. Overall, he had a nice body. I'm not completely shallow, but I found him very fuckable.

Fuck... Oh fuck. The impression I got was that he was just looking for a casual fuck.

Is it really a wise idea to call him?

After a few days, I couldn't stop thinking about Rick, if that was his name. Was I ready for a rebound fuck? Could I handle a rebound fuck? Sure, I was horny and I could use some dick. My fist was getting boring...

I pulled my phone out of my pocket and called Rick. I'm not a texter, I like talking.

Ring, ring, ring.

"Hello?" Rick said. *Holy fuck,* he actually answered the phone!

"Hey, it's me, Sam from the gym."

"Oh, hey Sam," he flirtatiously said, "I wasn't sure if I scared you away."

"Admittedly, you freaked me out," I huffed and tried not to sound awkward, "just a little."

He deeply laughed and said, "Alright then. Dinner at my place tonight. Six o'clock. I'll text you the address, don't be late."

After saying our goodbyes, we hung up. So, the stranger from the gym was trying to romance me a little bit before he fucked me. It was a thoughtful gesture and I was cool with it. Now that I thought about it, maybe I would fuck him. I couldn't wait to find out.

After pulling into his apartment complex, I walked to his front door. As I knocked on the door, my hands were sweating. I smelt good-food as the door opened.

I laughed, "Wow, you're actually cooking."

Then he waved me in. "Yes, of course. I am no Gordon Ramsey, but I can cook fairly well." I followed him to the kitchen table. "Sit here while I grab the food."

Fuck, I was nervous. I had no idea what to expect. There was more of a date feeling to this than just a casual fuck. He brought back two plates with chicken and asparagus.

"I'm trying to eat better since I'm working out," Rick said.

I sat here awkwardly watching him dig into his food. To be

polite, I took a bite.

"Damn, this is good," I said.

"Thanks," he said while wiping his face on a napkin.

"So, tell me about yourself. I literally only know your name," I said.

His eyes were serious as he looked at me. "Actually, there is something you need to know about me."

Oh fuck, is this the part where he tells me he's a serial killer or some crazy shit?

I gulped and said, "Okay."

"I've never had sex with a man before," he calmly said, like we were discussing the weather. Because I was choking on nothing, I'm glad there wasn't any food in my mouth.

"What? Did I hear that right?"

"You heard right." He casually cut his chicken and took a bite. "Just because I've never done it before doesn't mean that I don't want to."

"Fair enough."

The process of 'training' a straight man in bed can sometimes be challenging. I've only done it twice and vowed never to do it again. He would need to be prepped, shown how it's done. That's only if he doesn't get nervous or freak out. It wasn't fun dealing with the freakout moments... He was a complete stranger to me. The idea of being this man's bedroom guinea pig was a bit daunting to me.

I pushed my half eaten food out of the way. With as much sensitivity as I could muster, I spoke softly, "If you're just trying to explore your sexuality, you could always get some toys to practice with. Oh, and don't forget the lube. See if you like it first." My mouth was so fucking dry, I took a big gulp of water, then said, "Try that first before you bring a man into your bed."

He chuckled... I wasn't expecting him to laugh. It was a better reaction than I was expecting.

"Oh, I stuff myself with toys and have plenty of lube," he said, leaning forward and touching me. "You don't think I could handle a man like you in bed?"

In his eyes, there was a hint of challenge.

I accept the challenge.

"I suppose there's only one way to find out," I rasped.

He had more experience than I thought. The fact that he didn't have a completely untouched ass was a good thing—trust me.

He laughed and said, "Let's finish our food first. We have all night, there's no rush."

"You are a good cook," I complemented.

During our meal, we had some small talk. At least he wasn't a total stranger anymore. He told me about his school, his job. I'm having trouble remembering because all I could think of was dick...

Once we were finished eating, he got up and asked, "Shall we go to my bedroom?"

"Yes, let's go to your bed." I guess there won't be a couch make out session first. I wondered what sort of toys he was using on his ass, or if he would show me. Maybe he'll let me use one on him if I'm lucky.

Sitting on the edge of his bed, he took off his shoes and laid on his side.

"Are you going to join me or stand there?" he asked.

My dick was already getting a little hard... For some reason, I was kind of nervous. As soon as I sat on the bed, I took my shoes off.

"Your bed is comfortable," I said while thinking it was perfect for fucking. I decided to let him take the initiative. I'd let him lead since this was his first time experimenting with a man.

"Can I kiss you?" he asked.

"Yes."

Considering that he invited me to his bed, I thought he was very polite to ask. I was expecting him to charge at me like a wild animal.

He leaned forward and kissed me. I groaned as he playfully sucked my bottom lip into his mouth. Fuck, I groaned because it felt so good. For me, it's been a while, and I couldn't deny how good it felt. Especially when he sucked on my tongue. I don't even know how he did it. It would be great if that was my dick, but I'll get him there eventually.

We were fully making out; his tongue flicked around my mouth and fuck me, it was making my dick hard. I could hear him moaning and feel him putting his hands up my shirt.

My dick was already rock-hard, so I pressed it into his thigh. When I tried to press my dick on his, he was lying on his side at an angle that prevented me from doing it. He pulled away from our kiss.

"Can I see you naked?" he politely asked.

He was still fully clothed, but whatever. "Yes, you can."

I stood up and he gazed at me with rapt attention, his eyes glistening with lust. Then I took off my shirt, hoping he would like what he saw.

"Should I continue?" I asked.

"Yes. Please take your pants off."

I wasn't sure if I was giving him a peep-show or if we were going to have sex. It doesn't matter, I was here. I couldn't have sex with clothes on... As soon as I undid my button and zipper, I slid my boxers and pants off. My pants were around my ankles as I stood there. I wasn't sure if this was a good or bad thing when Rick stared at me with his jaw gaping open.

I felt awkward and said, "Um, should I pull them back up?" Dammit, my dick was hard... so hard I could hang a towel on it.

"No, please don't leave, stay. I'll get naked too."

Rick sat up and peeled off his shirt, then slid off his pants. I've never seen anyone strip so fast. His body was definitely nice. Also, a nice cock... and nice balls. A nice package was always a plus. I wasn't a size-queen, but he was pretty big.

I sat down on the edge of the bed. "We don't have to do anything you don't want to. But can I see your toys?" I really wanted to see how he'd been playing with himself. And I wanted to stuff him full of toys... Only if he'd let me.

His cheeks flushed red. "Sure." He walked to his dresser bare-assed. And fuck it was a nice ass. He dug around and pulled out a couple dildoes and a butt plug. The dildoes were decent-sized, one was green and the other was purple. His butt plug was black.

"Do you have any anal beads?" I asked. I wasn't sure if he even knew what that was.

"No, I don't."

"I'll buy some and next time, I'll blow your mind with them."

"Sounds good," he rasped and laid down on the bed with his toys.

"Can I put one inside you?" I cautiously asked and cocked an eyebrow.

"Yes, stick a toy in me and prep me before you fuck me. I want to be well prepared for my first time taking a real cock in my ass."

"It's my pleasure to prepare you and make you feel good with my dick."

I wanted to do so many things to this man. I wanted to suck him, fuck him, spank him… and so much more. But I would start with the purple dildo. I took his lube and put some in my palm and rubbed it up and down the shaft of the toy. I then stood at the end of the bed, and his legs were clamped shut.

I palmed his foot. "Open for me."

"Shit, okay," he rasped.

As he spread his legs wide open, my dick was already begging to be buried in his ass. My palms spread his legs wider as I got between them. My favorite view of a man is when his legs are wide open and ready to be fucked. I also loved the hair that coated the base of his dick and dusted his balls and his ass crack. It's true, I have a thing for body hair. Furry men have always been my favorite. Raking my fingernails (or the tip of my dick) through thick chest hair was fun.

I pulled his cheeks apart with one hand and found his pink puckering hole. I pressed the toy into the tight ring and he moaned. "Fuck that feels good, but I know your dick would feel better."

"Yes it will feel better, but let me stretch you first."

I pushed the toy in deeper, watching his hole stretch around the rubber dong. It was fucking sexy, but I wanted to see how he liked to play with himself. If I watched him, it would be easier for me to please him with my dick.

"You take over. Let me watch you."

"Fuck, alright." He reached for the toy and began pumping it in and out of his ass. I watched him slowly fuck himself, pushing it a little deeper each time.

"I want your dick now," he begged and pulled the toy out of his ass.

I got the condom from the back pocket of my pants.

"This is a ribbed rubber. I hope that's alright. It's all 7-eleven had."

"Oh fuck, that's going to feel good."

"Yes it will."

I rolled the condom down my shaft and made sure I had it on right. There's been a time or two when I rolled it down inside out.

I slid between his knees and aligned my head at his entrance. I pressed his knees open with my palms and pushed my hips forward. Rick's eyebrows scrunched and he was already panting and mumbling, "Oh f-fuck, that... dick... So good."

It was surprisingly easy to slide balls deep. He'd definitely been playing with himself. That was good, it made everything easier for me. I didn't have to worry so much about hurting him.

I thrust in and out of his virgin ass, and it was fucking bliss. "Take my dick."

I was slowly fucking him, just like the way he was playing with his toy.

"Yes... yes fuck me! Harder... faster!" he moaned.

As my pace quickened, I slammed into his ass. I was deep in his channel as he pushed his hips up to meet my thrusts. I was deep...

so deep inside him. I loved the sound of our bodies slamming together and the obnoxious sound of his loose headboard *tap, tap, tapping* on the wall. His neighbors would know he was getting some.

He fisted his dick and started jerking it. His hand slid up and down his shaft faster and faster. I was close to coming too. My nuts were tight and I felt the sensation that meant I was close. My dick was going to explode.

"I'm going to cum!" I shouted while nailing his ass.

"Mmm," he moaned and his dick began firing off, shooting all over his stomach and chest. He was wet, and sticky. There wasn't anything sexier than a man soaking in his own juices. For me, the only thing better was swallowing. Next time, I would drink him down.

I pulled my dick out of his ass and pressed our chests together. I didn't mind being wet and sticky so I could kiss him.

I broke our kiss and asked, "How was your first time?" That was such a loaded question. I shouldn't have asked that. For all I know, he could say I was a terrible fuck.

"Fucking amazing," he rasped.

I raked my hands nervously through my hair. "Glad to hear that. So, I'll hear from you later?"

He smiled, "Yes, of course."

It didn't take long to hear from Rick. It's the very next day and he's here in my bed.

"I want to suck your dick," I said while scraping my teeth on his neck. I then slapped his bare ass.

"Fuck ok," he deeply rasped.

"Stand up at the edge of my bed."

"Why?" he chuckled.

"It's better for deep-throating." I slapped his ass again. "Up you go."

He stood up, his cock jutting out ramrod straight. I slurped his wet head into my mouth. Fuck, I really loved the way he tasted. He trickled ample amounts of precum down the back of my throat. I grasped his ass cheeks and pushed him deeper in my mouth. Up and down I sucked his length and he caught on. He grabbed handfuls of my hair and face-fucked me. That's why I had him stand up. It was easier to show him you can get better leverage this way. He only has open air behind his ass, instead of a bed. He was slamming into my face and lucky for him... I didn't really have a gag reflex. I actually liked the feeling of a crown sinking into my throat.

"Oh God," he moaned, "I'm going to cum... I'm... fuck!"

His nuts were high and tight. Then I felt his warm cream pump into my mouth. He tasted so fucking good... Not overly salty or bitter. I couldn't begin to describe his taste. It was uniquely and naturally his own. Every man tastes differently, but his flavor was my favorite. I'd become addicted to drinking him down.

I sucked his balls completely dry.

"It's your turn," he purred.

"Damn, alright."

It was the most enthusiastic and sloppy blowjob of my life. I fucking loved it. He looked up at me proudly after he swallowed.

"Kiss me," I said. Call me nasty, but I liked to taste myself on a man's lips...

This became our nightly ritual. He'd come over and we would have sex. Tonight was going to be special though. I had something planned. But he insisted on sucking me off the moment he walked in my room. And of course I kissed him after.

We were kissing and suddenly I realized what a rude lover I was. I pulled away and said, "You didn't come yet."

"Nope, I didn't."

"I have a present for you."

His eyes widened with surprise. "Really?"

"Yes, really." I pulled out the package from my drawer. I ordered his gift online. I handed it to him and said, "Open it."

He tore open the white bubble cushioned package.

"Anal beads and lube!" he said with his cheeks flushing red.

"Want to try them?" *Please say yes.*

"Fuck yeah!"

"Get on all fours for me, elbows and knees on my bed." Sometimes, I could be a little bit of a dom.

He did what he was told and his ass was presented to me. It was there for me to play with and please. I really wanted to make him feel good. Just because I liked anal beads didn't mean he would…

I squirt the lube directly on his hole.

"Oh wow, my ass is wet!"

"It will feel better this way, trust me." I've done this to myself plenty of times to know it's not good when dry. The wetter the better, in my opinion. Although I didn't want to admit it out loud.

His ass was soaking wet and glistening with the oily lube. He was wet… so wet and warm. If I didn't come already, I'd bury my cock in his ass. But not now because it was about making him feel good.

I pushed the first bead in, I watched his hole swallow it. Then I pushed in another... and another. The plastic string of beads hanging out of his hole were wet with the dripping lube.

"You're so sexy, look at you. Do you like the way it feels?"

"Yes, oh fuck yes. Push some more in."

"Of course. Tell me when to stop."

One by one, I pushed the beads in and watched his star-shaped flesh swallow the beads. If he thought this felt good, my surprise wasn't over. Wait until I pulled them out! For some reason, that always got me off.

"Okay, leave them there," he moaned and started jerking his dick. I left the beads in place, but tugged on them lightly, just so he could feel the sensation.

"Holy f-fuck!" he moaned.

"When you're about to cum, tell me. I'm going to pull them out when you're coming. You're going to love it, trust me."

The wet lube dripped from his hole, down the back of his balls. I saw him wipe some lube off his balls and on his shaft. He stroked his cock with a quick pace.

"Oh fuck, I'm going to cum!"

I saw his toes curling—he always did that when he was about to blow his load.

So, I pulled the beads out much quicker then I slid them in.

"Oh fuck!" he cried out. "That feels… so good!" he rasped while he came, blowing his load onto my bed sheets.

He collapsed on his stomach. He was a breathless, sticky wet mess. I'd get him to the shower, cleaned up and in bed with me tonight where he belonged.

The end

CAUGHT

Straight to gay

Kyle Rayne

CAUGHT

Straight to gay

Kyle Rayne

There are times when I look at men sexually. What the fuck does that mean? I don't think I'm... I won't even say it. It's just that I've only fucked women and I'd be lying if I said I didn't picture myself sleeping with someone else when I close my eyes. Not just anyone... My best friend Alex.

Since I was a child, I knew he was gay. Our friendship dates back to middle school. I figured out he was gay pretty quick, and to be honest, I didn't care. He's *never* hit on me and has always been respectful.

His breakups are the only thing that bothers me about his relationships. Whenever he needs comfort, I'm there for him. Once, he cried on my shoulder, and if I ever mention it, he'll punch me. According to him, it never happened. That's fine with me, since I hate talking about feelings and shit. It's for this reason that I'm a little discombobulated whenever I think about him. Things are stirring deep in my belly... and lower down.

It makes my dick twitch when I think about him in the shower. It's something about the way he looks and smells. That's fucking weird, isn't it? There's something about his scent that's uniquely his. When he wasn't looking, I might have sniffed his pillow...

I'm masturbating full-throttle right now. It's Alex assaulting my fantasies. My fantasy isn't just about him—it's both of us. I'm already close as I slide my fist up and down my length. I'm imagining that I'm sucking his dick. I fantasize my lips wrapped around his length.

Water pelted my dick when I jerked it. "Oh God, Alex, " I moaned to myself.

Then I imagine myself fucking his ass. Or him fucking me. Since I've never tried it... I don't know what I prefer... That fantasy gives me an idea. With one hand, I jerk my dick and with the other, I reach behind my ass and find my hole. I push my finger on my hole, but I don't insert it. The pressure feels amazing! I am still playing with my untouched area...

"Oh, fucking fuck, that feels good." I'm not talking to anyone.

Suddenly, I realize how difficult it is to stroke my dick and finger my ass at the same time. I would appreciate an extra pair of hands or a dick.

This time, I press my finger in a little deeper. It feels so good, it pushes me over the edge. As my nuts hug up tight, my load shoots into the shower.

"Oh fuck Alex!" I moan so loudly that I almost scream.

Suddenly, I hear a light rapping at my bathroom door. "What the fuck Ben?"

Oh. My. God. I can't believe it's Alex. He didn't tell me he was coming over. For years, he has had a key to my apartment.

Before I opened my bathroom door, I wrapped a towel around my waist. Alex stood in front of my bathroom door with his arms crossed. The way his eyebrows were scrunched was his 'tell.' I knew he was worried.

I'm not sure if he knows I was masturbating and thinking about him. I guess he didn't hear me?

"What are you doing here?" I asked.

Taking a look at his watch, he taps it. "I told you I would be here at four. We're going to the movies."

"Oh, yeah. Now I remember."

When he's single, he always does this to me. We go out platonically—dinner, movies. I don't want to do it anymore for some reason. I don't feel right about it. He always uses me as a pawn until he finds a new partner. After that, he forgets about me…

Putting my hands on his shoulders, I said, "Listen Alex. We need to talk."

"Okay. What's up?"

He looked hurt when I said, "I don't want to go tonight." My guess is he didn't hear me stroking my dick and screaming his name.

"Would you like to watch a movie here?" he asked.

Tonight, I didn't want to watch a movie... Unless it was with my lover/partner, which he wasn't. I wanted to spend time with someone who wasn't just using me as a convenient rebound buddy.

My hands raked through my wet hair and down my freshly shaved face.

It was difficult to find the words to say. "Alex. I... um."

"There's no point in spending time with you, if you don't want me here." He turned around and stormed off.

"Wait," I said, "let's spend some time together."

Get some fucking balls and tell him how you feel.

Over his shoulder, he glanced at me.

"I can't be your friend only when you're fucking single!" I shouted. It was as if flood gates opened in my heart. Now I couldn't stop myself... "It's unfair you want me only when you're conveniently single. When you find someone, I don't hear from you for months." My heart was beating so loudly that I wondered if he could hear it.

His eyes were fixed on me in a way he'd never looked at me before.

"Ben, what are you saying? Are you..." he trailed off.

In the end, he didn't finish his question. Since we've been friends for so long, he was reluctant to cross that barrier. We couldn't go back once we crossed that barrier. It was my dream to cross this barrier. This friendship wasn't enough for me. That's what I wanted...

"I really want you, okay?" With my fists balled, I shouted, "I fucking want you. I just don't want to be at your beck and call."

There was a ghostly whiteness to his normally dark cheeks. Yeah, I fucked up, my friend is gone. All he did was stare at me.

"Say fucking something," I rasped.

I kept my gaze on him the entire time.

"Never mind, I don't care. I'll be here when it's convenient for you. Let's go to your movie tonight. When you get another partner, you can forget about me. We'll keep doing what we've always done."

His jaw gaped open before he finally whispered, "I didn't realize you had feelings for me."

"What, how could you not know?" I shouted.

Alex remained silent... speechless. While I had only a towel on, he stared at me and I was about to punch him. I walked to my bedroom and said, "Just leave. I don't need you to stare at my nearly-naked body."

"Ben, I want you to," he whispered softly, but I heard him. Taking a step closer, he said, "I've wanted you for so long, although I'd never hit on you. You should know that. As a gay guy, I don't hit on my straight friends."

I was about to get dressed. If I kept the towel on, maybe he would get me naked.

It's been my dream for so long to have this moment, so I bravely said, "Kiss me."

"Fuck, okay."

Alex wrapped his arms around my neck and I inhaled his scent, which made my dick start to get hard. I groaned as he pressed his hips against mine. My tongue slipped into his mouth, and I moaned. My fantasy was nothing compared to the real thing. My hips pressed against his jeans.

Only a wet towel separated my dick from his jeans.

I wanted to know if he had a hard on for me. I pushed my hips against his. There was some wood sprouting, dammit. The blood was already trickling up my dick even though I just jacked-off in the shower.

The next thing I knew, Alex was kissing me and pushing me backwards. I lost my towel when we were stumbling to my bed—perfect!

I was completely naked for Alex when he shoved me onto my bed. Damn, he was a little aggressive and it just made me more attracted to him. I was turned on even more because of it. I've never seen this side of him before.

It was like he was drinking me in with his eyes.

He purred, "Look at how sexy you are."

My dick stood ramrod straight, and I felt completely exposed.

"It's time to get naked. We can't have sex if you're dressed," I blurted out.

"You want to have sex with me?"

"Don't play coy. Yes, I want to have sex with you."

"Ok, I'll get naked for you."

He removed his jacket and placed it on my dresser. He undressed too slowly. I got up and pulled his shirt over his head. I've seen him without his shirt before, but *this* was different. *This* was sexual.

As I unzipped his jeans, I kissed him. Our kiss was a mess of tongue and teeth, he kissed aggressively and passionately.

I didn't hesitate to pull down his boxers. In the midst of kissing him, I glanced down. Fuck, he has a nice dick. The crown of his head was flushed red and his shaft was lined with purple veins.

My lips pulled away from his.

"Damn, you have a porn-star dick," I teased.

"You've been watching gay porn?" he questioned.

"Well, yeah, Don't you watch porn?" I said without shame.

"Only when I'm single and desperate for sex. Looks like you'll take care of that for me," he rasped.

I knew Ben well enough to know this wasn't a one-time thing. But enough thinking... let's start with sex.

Our dicks were grinding together as we stood there kissing again. Oh my fuck, that felt better than I could have imagined. It wouldn't get me off, but I didn't want to rush anyway.

After sliding my hands down his chest and abdomen, I reached the base of his dick. As my hand rested there, I didn't touch him.

"Can I touch your cock?" I asked.

I thought I should probably ask, even though we were naked with our swords crossed.

"Yes. Can I touch yours?" he asked, breathing heavily.

"Fuck yes. Please," I rasped.

The two of us were stroking each other's cocks while standing up. It was fucking amazing to explore another man's body. He wasn't just any man, he was my best friend and now he was my lover.

I wanted to touch him elsewhere. There was so much I wanted to touch. In the meantime, I was happy massaging his balls and cupping his sac. My mind was blown and engrossed in the moment.

"Wouldn't your bed be better than standing?" Alex asked.

"It would, yes. Although I'd fuck you in an airplane bathroom or the backseat of a car. I don't care where we are, I just want you."

I was overcome with sudden desperation for him that I'd been suppressing. Suddenly, I was ravenous for his dick.

I grabbed his shoulders and shoved him on my bed. There was no way I wasn't going to lick every inch of his body. He was going to get a mouthful of me. His dick was jutting up in the air, his slit glistening with precum

"I'm going to taste you everywhere," I rasped as I pushed his legs apart. "Put my pillow under your ass."

There was a red flush on his cheeks. "What did you have in mind?" he asked while shoving my pillow under his ass.

"I'm going to lick you." I dropped to my knees and placed his legs over my shoulders. With my fingers, I parted his crack. Then I spread him wide and found what I desperately wanted.

"Are you sure?" he coyly asked.

"I've eaten enough pussy to figure out how to make you feel good."

To silence him, I dove face first into his crack. As I lifted his heavy sac, I cupped it in my hands. I licked his balls, all the way down his taint and pressed my tongue into his ass.

"Oh fuck," he moaned and scrunched his eyes.

That was a good sign—I was making him feel good. I licked him in a straight line from his balls to his hole again, then I plunged my tongue into his hole.

"Oh baby, that feels so fucking good," he moaned.

When I really started working my tongue into him, his cheeks flushed red and his eyebrows scrunched. I couldn't wait to see his cum-face. It would be fucking epic. I've always wondered what it looked like...

I spit on his hole to keep it moist. I had lube, but for what I was about to do, this was good enough. I slipped my pointer finger into his ass. I dragged it in and out. I wasn't sure if I'd fuck him tonight, but I just wanted to get to know if better sexually and make him feel good. I was determined to be the best fuck he'd ever had.

While propped up on my elbows, I sucked his glistening crown into my mouth.

"Oh my fucking G-god," he moaned and ran his hands through my hair. He gently pushed my head down his length with both hands resting on the back of my head.

As I fingered his hole, I sucked his length up and down. The moaning told me he was feeling good, but I wanted our first time to be special.

I spit his dick out and asked, "Is this going to make you come, baby? Tell me what else to do."

"I want… I want you inside me," he quietly said.

The next time I would get him to fuck me, because I wanted him inside me. At the moment, it was all about my best friend and making him feel good. My goal was to keep him in my bed and away from shitty partners. Now I was going to keep him all to myself. The next time we went to the movies, it would be a date night. No more 'bro-outings.' I wanted so much more than just to make him cum.

"Fuck, okay. Whatever you want," I said.

From my nightstand, I grabbed some lube and squirted it into my palm. I rubbed it all over my shaft.

"Don't make fun of me because I'm a rookie. Do I need to, um, do anything else to prep you?" I felt my cheeks flush red with embarrassment.

"No, you warmed me up with your fingers and tongue just fine. I want it doggy style," he rasped and flipped over on all fours.

I never realized how sexy he was, especially now that he is fully prepared to be fucked. After getting between his knees, I aligned my dick at his hole. It was pinkish-brown and puckering for me. His fucking ass... it was so sexy. In a stark moment of clarity—or an epiphany—I can't believe I ever thought I was straight. Straight people probably don't need to spend so much time convincing themselves that they're straight.

I pushed my head into his flesh—his tight ring of muscle was swallowing my dick completely. I inched in slowly and it felt so fucking good. I slid my dick completely in until I was balls deep.

He fisted my bedsheets and shoved his face into the mattress.

"Oh fuck, your dick feels so fucking good. You're so thick," he rasped.

A sudden immature jealousy stung me—I didn't want to know how many guys he said that too.

"Can I fuck you now?" I asked.

"Yes, please fuck me. I *need* you to fuck me."

I was dragging my dick in and out of his ass at a good pace. I wanted to know how he liked to get fucked.

"Should I go slow, or fast?"

"Faster... please fuck me faster," he begged.

That was all I needed to hear. I looked down and watched my dick slide in and out of his ass.

It felt so fucking good... his warm flesh engulfed my cock.

I was fucking him as fast as I could. I loved the sound of my hips slamming against his cheeks. All of it... It was so fucking sexy. My dick in my best friend's ass. My nuts started to tingle, and I knew I was close. I was going to cum.

"I... I want you to cum first," I rasped and leaned forward and reached around and fisted his cock. I jerked his dick the way I liked it. I didn't put too much pressure on his shaft.

"Oh my fucking... oh Ben!" He moaned my name drenched with lust. It was the sexiest thing I've heard escape his lips. So, I jerked his dick faster so he could moan my name all night long.

"Ben, I'm coming!" he deeply rasped.

He was spilling his load onto my bedsheets.

When he moaned my name, I couldn't handle it. It was sending shockwaves through my brain, all the way down to my dick. I was going to cum.

His hole was quivering around my shaft. From my nuts to my dick, I started pumping my load into his ass. I was deep, deep inside him, pumping him full of my cum.

"Fuck, Alex," I rasped.

It was the most intense orgasm of my life! The best part... I'll never fuck a pussy again. It wasn't for me anymore, but I didn't have anything against it. I wouldn't be satisfied fucking a woman in the ass. Dick... and balls... I liked them both.

My cum was spilling out as I pulled my dick out of his ass. Why was that so fucking hot? I'd never get tired of seeing that. My best friend and lover, bent over moaning my name.

I patted his ass. "Come on, let's go shower."

His cheeks flushed a deeper shade of red. "We're going to shower together?"

"Um, yeah. This ain't some one night stand bullshit. Come on."

After the water got warm, we stepped into my shower. I squirted my body wash into his palm.

"You can stand under the water first. I bet you want to clean yourself out."

I watched him spread his cheeks and the water splash off his ass. It felt so intimate watching him. From now on, I'd be the only man to see him this intimately.

"We can make it to the nine o'clock showing. We're going to dinner first," I said to Alex and kissed him on the cheek. "But this is our first real date. I want hand holding and the full nine yards."

"Really?" he asked.

Was I being too pushy? I didn't think so. He's the longest friend I've ever had. There was a sense that I deserved it.

"Yes really. Unless you are just planning to keep me as your dirty little secret."

As I waited for an answer, my heart sank. After turning off the water, I reached for a pair of towels on the rack.

"You're not my *dirty* little secret. If you are ready to come out, and publicly before you've told anyone. There's a chance we could run into someone we know."

"I'm ready."

It was nice going out for dinner and watching a movie as a couple. I haven't had a real date in so fucking long. The best part was that there was no awkwardness. Since we already knew each other, there were no weird or unfamiliar questions. I felt like he had always belonged with me.

"Let's spend the night at my place," Alex said as we left the movie theater, and I couldn't be happier. He hasn't invited me to sleep over since high school. Back then, I slept on a squeaky air mattress that was flat by morning.

"Okay baby," I said and kissed his cheek.

There were some people who weren't used to men showing PDA

in public--Fuck them. We wouldn't even be noticed if we were a male/female couple. I don't care what they think. Alex was probably used to it.

We cuddled up in his bed at his place.

"Damn, your bed is comfortable." I've sat on it, but I've never slept in it.

"It's more comfortable with you in it," he said, wrapping his arms around me.

As he pressed against me, his body was so warm and he felt so good. I felt my dick pump up. It was twitching, and dammit, I couldn't hide it since we were both naked. I pressed my dick into his thigh. Since I had already fucked him senseless, I didn't know if he was in the mood. Maybe we could reverse roles... I wanted to be on the bottom.

"Damn Ben. You're ready for round number two?" he shyly asked.

"I am, but this time, I want to try something different."

"Really?" he asked in a deep, husky voice.

"Yes. I want you to fuck me in my ass."

"Damn, ok. Let me get my lube."

"Prep me with your fingers first."

"Of course," he purred.

Next thing I knew, both of my feet were up in the air while he fucked me deep, hard and slow. His dick in my ass was the best thing I've ever experienced.

"How do you like getting fucked?" Alex asked.

"I fucking love it," I moaned. I would never get enough of his dick.

"Fuck me hard. I want it hard. You won't break me."

"Whatever you want."

As he slammed into me and nailed my hole, I knew I would be sore tomorrow. I'd probably be sore for a couple days, but it's worth it. Walking around, *that* would feel like our dirty little secret that only we shared.

By the time we were done, we were both sticky with sweat, cum and lube—it was perfect.

"Hey Alex. Did you hear anything unusual when you knocked on my bathroom door?"

"I thought you were moaning my name. I figured it was my imagination so I didn't say anything."

"Well, you caught me. You've been a fixation in my shower jerk-off fantasies for a while."

The end

SEDUCTION

Straight to gay

Kyle Rayne

G rowing up in the lower class, not many have the means or the finances to pay their way into higher education. The lucky ones have their brains to achieve scholarships and acceptance letters. Others, like myself, are born with a physic that paves the way to success.

Throughout my education, I kept my grades high and worked even harder on the field. I received above average marks in high school that continued at the local college I attended. The years of effort I put in paid off when a coach from my state's university attended one of our games. Before I knew it, I had signed a scholarship that would change my life.

I settled in well and hit it off with my new teammates, which were a rowdy bunch of guys especially the quarterback, Brad. He was the life of the party, but, once on the field, it was like flipping a switch and his happy go lucky attitude became serious. When the ball was in his hands, it was like nothing could stop him. Of course, there were bad days when he would be stopped by an intervening player or another variant that could ruin a game. After a loss by his fault or another's, he never soured but, instead, would give the team pep talks that even the coach couldn't match. Without him, we wouldn't be as successful as we are now.

Despite being a team player, he was a jokester who seemed to have something on everyone to use against them; all in good fun. After a time, I noticed he thoroughly enjoyed teasing me. It started off with casual comments off the field with how well I played. On the field he would pat me on the ass just like all the others on the team, but it felt like his hand would linger just a bit too long. In the locker room, he took to hiding my towel and my clothing. (I can't tell you how many times I had to walk around with my ass out searching.)

Now, I'm not a straight chaser, but that doesn't mean I don't notice when a man makes a pass or use childish tactics to shroud their desires. His actions reminded me of a schoolboy who liked a girl and didn't understand how to express himself to, however I passed off his feats as him being mischievous. What was I supposed to think when he would talk about the various women he had relations with? Even more so when he would introduce his new girlfriends, which never lasted long and were the stereotypical kind to be on the arm of a quarterback.

All my questioning came to a head while the team was getting ready for the next training session. We were in the locker room putting our gear on and one by one heading out to line up. I arrived late due to ill timing on my part and was well behind the rest. My locker just opened when Brad came in, and he appeared distraught as he flung his training bag on the bench.

"You alright?" I asked, seeing as he was not himself.

"Yeah," he huffed then shook his head. "No, actually, not really."

"Lady troubles…?"

"Always!" He tossed his clothing in the locker in anger then added, "I don't get how girls think. They go believing one thing and a single comment will change everything."

"That they do," I agreed. "Might have better luck dating a girl with more brains than tits."

Brad laughed. "You think? Are brains better than tits in your experience?"

I bit my tongue for moment, shuffling through my clothes before answering sarcastically with, "Better in mine among other things."

"So, what is your taste in women? Haven't seen you with a lady since joining."

"Haven't found the right partner."

An eyebrow of his cocked at me as he leaned in close. "'Partner…?' What's that supposed to mean?" he inquired.

My eyes rolled instinctively. "It means what I said: haven't met someone worth the effort."

Brad's eyes narrowed at me then relaxed. "Wish I had your patience," he praised with a shrug. "I can't seem to keep my dick in my pants."

"That's for sure," I concurred with a laugh. "You'll find the right girl that rides you like she treats you."

"Do you like to ride?"

"What's *that* supposed to mean?"

"I don't know, Damon." A smirk came to his lips before he continued, "Haven't seen a girl on your arm and you give vague genderless advice... Might make one think you like batting for the same team."

I stared at him, not quite sure how to respond. Before I knew it, my words had no trace of thought behind them. To make it even worse, my behavior followed suit.

"*You* should try batting for the same team."

Brad froze in place as my lips met his. His hands went to the sides of my arms, and I just knew he was going to resist, but, surprisingly, he didn't push me away. He kissed back while his hands tightened on my arms and felt like he wanted to pull me closer instead. We shared a kiss that only lasted several moments but it seemed like hours. Just when his tongue passed my lips did Brad step back, breaking our exchange. There was shock and confusion on his face as we stared at one another.

"Damon, I'm not... I don't—"

Remembering myself and feeling like I made a mistake, I interrupted him, "I'm sorry, Brad... I don't know what I was thinking... Bad joke..."

"Yeah," Brad slowly nodded his head, "bad joke. Um, we should —" he looked around the locker room as if someone might have seen us, "—we should get out there. Coach is probably pissed."

"He's probably livid," I said and finished changing.

Honestly, I assumed Brad was going to completely turn on me after that. I expected the others to find out about it since he was the type to have the gall to tell the rest their co-player made a pass at him. The dynamics of the team could have been ruined by my action. My thoughts darkened, sending me into a downward spiral, the more I contemplated over the ruined future.

As the weeks went on, Brad continued being his happy-go-lucky self, however I noticed how much he badgered me dwindled. I didn't have to go search for my clothes or be subjected to the next round of towel whipping. He also stopped talking about his ever-rotating girlfriends. It made me wonder if he took my initial advice in finding someone better than just the next empty shell.

It seemed like what happened between us would stay that way and nothing more. I should have been grateful for his discretion but found myself disappointed in its place. I kept pondering why he kissed me back. Most straight men would have been disgusted at the first move let alone enraged, yet he was passive and kept what happened to himself.

My education challenged me more as the year moved on while practices were extended as we won game after game since the coach didn't want us going soft due to the victories. Balancing the two dwarfed my personal life, unfortunately. If my face wasn't buried in a book, it was stuffed into a helmet. Having so much to do was daunting, but I enjoyed the constant flow of tasks even if the only reprieve I got was when my head hit the pillow.

Of course, my routine did have its draw backs, like not being able to relieve myself as every person needs to. I bottled my hormones up to the best of my capabilities, though keeping my own inhibitions to myself was difficult in a locker-room. A towel alone wasn't always enough to hide my excitement at their godlike figures, particularly around Brad. I found myself fantasizing about him more often than not. Little did I know my imagination would become reality.

One night we trained far longer than the coach meant to keep us. I anticipated the rest of the team to be showering and teasing one another as always. Apparently it was late enough that they didn't care to and went their separate ways. Seeing as I was the only one left, I figured washing in a space larger than a living room was preferable than to wait for a cramped shower in my dormitory.

The water was nice and hot compared to normal and I felt at

peace washing alone as having a group of men around made it difficult to enjoy the sanctity of bathing. It wasn't long before my state of mind was shattered due to a locker closing outside the showers. I covered myself out of instinct in a public space for a moment before remembering where I was. Turning to the entrance, surprise filled my expression as to who was entering.

"You're here late," I greeted Brad as he sauntered in fully exposed.

The man shrugged as he turned the dial next to mine. "Coach needed a word," he said. "I doubt the man ever stops thinking about tactics."

I stood there, trying not to stare at his perfect body. The outlines of his muscles strained against his own skin and water fell down his body like streams down a mountain. Urges to touch overwhelmed me, causing me to grip my bar of soap tighter.

"From what I've heard he's only got two interests in life."

"Yeah…? What are those?"

"Sports," a smile appeared on my lips, "and his wife."

"She's got a great sense of patience then," he replied with a smile. "Doubt she doesn't get any action until midnight."

I couldn't help what came out of my mouth next. "Have you been getting any action? Haven't heard you complaining about a girl in a while."

Brad briefly fell silent while his eyes flickered to and from me. "No, not really." He took a breath before adding, "Practice has been getting in the way of that. It's like the coach doesn't want us to have a social life outside the field."

"Ain't that the truth..."

Running water filled the air as the atmosphere became awkward. I wanted to talk to him more but found nothing worth conversating other than bringing up the past. Talking to him about it would probably help, yet I couldn't bring myself to mention it. The words were stuck in my throat.

"Have you gotten any?" he inquired with a strange face I couldn't understand.

"No, too busy just like you. I blame the coach."

A chuckle escaped as he said, "He's a good excuse."

The man wasn't washing himself at this point. The thoughts he had were more important than washing the sweat from his divine body. He then looked at me and a sinking feeling passed through me while my heart raced. Despite how uneasy I felt, I couldn't look away from him.

"Damon, I need—I want... I want to talk to you about what happened...between us..."

"I'm sorry, Brad, I shouldn't have done that."

"That's why I wanted to talk to you about it."

"You don't have to if you don't want to."

Brad shook his head as he said, "No, we need to." He shifted his stance, looking uncertain. "I didn't expect that from you, but, honestly, I can't stop thinking about it."

"Neither can I."

I looked at the other man expectantly, waiting for him to say something—*anything*. Brad stared back at me with his mouth open, ready to speak, but not even a croak sounded. A storm swirled around within his head as his face contorted. He was having difficulty with piecing his words together, which made it easy to tell he was frustrated with himself.

"Shit, you know I'm not one to beat around the bush..." He frowned as he released a huff and gritted his teeth "Its way easier talking to girls about this...but when I think about talking to you I find myself...choking."

"What do you mean?" I asked while my eyebrows knitted together, trying not to confuse myself with my own mind as it backtracked.

"What I mean is... What I'm trying to get at is..." He eyed me up and down, biting his lower lip. "Ah, fuck it."

My eyes widened as he approached me. In a single movement his hands were cupping my face and his lips were on mine. I stood my ground, accepting his advance and returning the kiss. As our lips move against one another, the bar of soap dropped my hands before they were placed on either side of his hips. One of Brad's limbs moved to hold the back of my head while the other went around my shoulder to bring me closer. His hold over me was so secure I couldn't move away from him as touches began to wander along the body below them.

He suddenly broke our kiss, causing us to gaze into each other's eye. I deliberated if we were going to make the dive, though he made the decision faster than I could. He pushed me up against a cold, wet wall that sent shivers through my body. Lips met again, and I felt his tongue desiring access, so I obliged. Our tongues battled for dominance, but it wasn't long before Brad claimed victory.

Finding a hold on him, I switched places with the other man. Brad's breathing hitched when I moved to his neck and nipped the skin just under his jaw before travelling down. It was hard not to note how sensitive the area was and how he writhed against me while our excitement ground against one another. Feeling the size of him against my own was more anticipation than I could handle. My second head took over at this point and I pulled back from his neck to glimpse at our cocks then back to meet his gaze. Knowing what I was after, he gave a nod and I barely caught sight of a smile as I dropped to my knees.

Seeing his dick right in front of me and at full length, I knew I had my work cut out for me as it was longer than mine and thick like a Red Bull can. I started at the base of his cock then worked the sides of his length while Brad laid a hand on my head while the other rested on my shoulder. Popping the head of his cock in my mouth, I fully realized I couldn't fit all of him down my throat. Previous experiences trained my gag reflex, but this was testing it. Nonetheless, I sucked his cock with skill, and the sounds coming out of his mouth made me curious if I was better, if not comparable, to the women he'd been with.

His hands went under my arms after some time and lifted me up. He kissed me frantically before switching places again. This time my front was against the wall with Brad pressing himself between the cheeks. He ground his cock into me, making me fear he was going to shove it inside me without any prep. Opening my mouth to speak, I felt him retreat then bury his face into my ass. The words I had were lost and turned into a moan as my brain caught up.

Brad pulled back when he heard me to ask rhetorically, "You like that?"

"Do you?"

With a chuckle, he said, "You may be my first guy, but I've eaten plenty of ass before."

I could feel his tongue pushing deeper into me as the muscles relaxed after he went back for more. The man was true to his word as I couldn't remember the last time I had my ass eaten out so well and rocked my hips against him. His hands, which were on my hips, held me tighter as the anticipation building between us was evident now more than ever.

He gave one final lick to my entrance before rising to whisper in my ear, "I'm going to fuck you."

Shivers racked my being as I warned him, "Water isn't a good lubricant."

"I can solve that." He nipped at my ear and turned me around, pecking my lips. "I've got some lube in my bag."

"You've got lube?"

"I come prepared in case I hook up with a kinky girl," he replied with a sly smile.

A laugh escaped from me as I shook my head.

Since Brad's bag was outside the showers, instead of just

following him to it, we kissed, fondled, and nipped at each other on the way. I laid myself down on the bench with haste upon arrival, positioning my ass in the air as he found his bottle of lube. It wasn't long before his length was lathered, and he fingered me briefly. As he pressed the head of his member against me, I was grateful of his knowledge as he eased his way into me.

The head of his cock stretched my hole and I groaned as he pushed inch after inch into me. His hands went to my waist to aid in nudging me backwards before he pulled out just enough to push in deeper. Once he was far enough, he picked up a rhythm that had me squirming beneath him. I held onto the sides of the bench as he dominated me, and I felt myself fully submit to him. When his hips pressed firmly against my ass, he stuffed me full of his cock and initiated a grunt to escape each of us. Taking full control now, he plowed into me like any other piece of ass.

As I bounced against him rapidly, I couldn't help but relish the feeling of him sliding in and out of me. The hold he had on my hips was secure as if making sure I wouldn't be able to get away from. Brad then slapped my ass, picking up his pace.

"Fuck...your ass is so good. Fuck, Damon..."

"Yeah...? You like your cock in my ass? Shit, you're so big..."

"Better be the biggest dick you've ridden," Brad said with pride. "Damn it," his tone changed, "I don't know how long—Damon,

I'm gonna cum."

"Do it," I panted. "Cum in my ass!"

"Fuck, here it comes!"

He stuffed me full of his cock again as he gripped my waist even tighter, and I could feel his cock pulsing inside of me. As he throbbed within me, I felt his seed coating my insides. Brad offered shallow thrusts like he was making sure to leave himself deep within. When he was done, he jiggled my cheeks while he pulled out, and I couldn't stifle the sounds of disproval I made.

He breathed heavily then took a step away from me. I slowly got up and felt my ass drip as we locked eyes and laughed. Brad kissed me deeply followed by grabbing my hard-on.

"Did you cum?"

"No."

He looked at me curiously then down at my cock. I held myself still feeling his lips tentatively wrap around me after he lowered himself. The feeling of his mouth covering my dick was more than I could have hoped for.

Brad didn't have a reason to train his gag reflex and it showed as he would choke and cough on my length, but he didn't shy away from me. His hands grabbed onto my ass for leverage as he continued and every moment that passed was like a lesson he was understanding. At one point, he surprised me by taking me all at once only to choke like a virgin. He came off my dick and gasped before putting it back in his mouth. Regardless, it was sooner than later that I couldn't hold back any longer.

My negligence in telling him I was cumming caught him off-guard as I held his head in place when I climaxed. Several jets of cum splashed in his mouth before he flung himself from me. He coughed and spat my seed out while I landed on the bench, feeling the aftereffects of a climax taking hold. I stared at the other man in disbelief of what happened between us as our lust settled.

"Fuck, that's nasty," Brad commented wiping his mouth. "Not that you're—"

"No, I get it. Cum isn't for everyone, especially a virgin."

"I'm *not* a virgin."

"Not anymore. Now you've had both genders," I retorted with a devilish smile.

He shook his head with an amused huff. "Fair enough." Eyeing me with consideration, he continued with, "Not going to lie, this was great."

"Agreed, if not surprising and brief."

"Sorry. Usually I last much longer than that, but believe me, even I'm surprised. I never would have thought about doing something like this before you kissed me."

"I'm glad I kissed you then." I gave him a warm smile.

Brad returned the gesture with a glint in his eyes and said, "Me too."

TRYST

Straight to gay

Kyle Rayne

I never would have guessed what was in store for me after our tryst in the locker room. Brad made it clear he couldn't get enough of me, and I don't regret it, but...my ass has been tender for the last few months since. All because of him. When we were in either of our dormitories, I was like a new toy for him to amuse himself with. The man would have me bent over the desk with his face in my ass faster than the door could close. Sometimes, he would see how many fingers he could put inside me without going into fisting. Nonetheless, his cock would then be in my ass no sooner than his tongue or digits left my hole with a grip on my hips that was like being locked into a fuck machine. Once his cock was inside me, he didn't dare come out until he was finished. He would pull my hair, bite my neck, and choke me as he would keep up his rough rhythm into me. In all honesty, if his dick was in me to keep me with a dumb face (which thankfully he never saw) and state, I would submit to anything he wanted to do.

Now, Brad made it very clear from the get-go that he wanted to keep things discreet. Despite this, he couldn't keep it in his pants and seemed to like to test the limits of what we could get away with (e.g., randomly making out in the locker room right before practice, a blow job in the bathroom stall before class, and/or a quickie). The stipulation got in the way of a lot more fun the two of us could have been taking advantage of, but I still found myself wanting to spend more time with him. From what I could tell so was he as he would linger around, repeating that he needed to leave while stealing extra kisses.

Luckily for me, when I suggested making time for us by hiding away for a few days, Brad was on board. Finding an Airbnb within our price range was easy enough and the location wasn't too bad either, though we had to wait for the opportune time given that we couldn't ignore our responsibilities. It was a while before the coach decided to suspend practice for a weekend to give us all a reprieve from all the hard work we were putting in. Regardless of his reason, the team was ecstatic.

There was a bit of a complication that nearly threw a wrench in our plans. Our team threw together a last-minute party during that weekend at a hosting fraternity. Getting out of the party was easy for me since I declined to go to most parties if only to have a reprieve from the group of people I surrounded myself with. A simple, "Sorry, not this time," was enough to deter the guys from pressing. They tried enough when I first joined to know their words would fall on deaf ears.

Brad, on the other hand, lied his way out of it while also putting in some truth to it. I fought a blush when he told the guys he was going to be out of town and burying his face in some ass. They hooted and clapped him on the back while asking all the naughty questions, like how big "her" breasts were and if "she" had a fat ass. One inquired if anyone there knew her. I glared at him when he glanced at me only to snicker like a child and tell them they wouldn't.

As the week droned on, Brad would talk about how he was going to fuck me on every inch of the lodging. I jokingly suggested we abstain from one another until then, but he took it literally and made a bet. He said if I were to cum first, I had to suck him awake both mornings of our stay (not like I wasn't going to anyways).

I laughed it off and threw back, "If you cum first, I get to fuck *your* ass."

He stared at me, his smile dropping for only a moment. He gave me a nod, saying before capturing my lips for a kiss, "You're on."

When the weekend finally came, we left as soon as we could. We arrived separately as to maintain the air of caution, of course. Upon arrival, it caught me off guard to see that Brad was already there and inside, but the thought was quickly pushed away as I took in the area. It was a quaint studio apartment in the backyard of someone's property with street parking but a private, stone walkway to the unit. The path was lit by cute little lanterns and the well-maintained garden around made it feel like one was taking a walk through a fairy's garden.

I put in the code given by the host into the door and stepped inside to the sound of food cooking. Dropping my bag off at the door, I found a table pressed against a wall and set for two with a freshly lit table candle burning in the center. It was set too nicely, so I doubted Brad was the one to have made the gesture. He was, however, in the small kitchen cooking something that smelled delicious.

"Whatchya doin'?" I asked, leaning against the wall separating the kitchen from the rest of the studio.

Brad looked up from the stovetop and smiled when his eyes met mine. He didn't answer right away as he took a step over to kiss me like he was welcoming me home. I could feel my face warm up due to a blush as he did.

"I realized I never wined and dined you. We've gone straight to the dinning part every time." He turned his head trying to get a better view of my ass before adding, "I got here early so I can make you something and expose my cooking skills."

"'Expose your cooking skills?'" I repeated questionably.

"When have I ever said I could cook?" he retorted with a smirk.

"Never."

"Exactly. Don't tell the guys, but I took culinary throughout high school."

"You did...?"

I couldn't believe him. Never would I have guessed he could cook or take classes. Not to mention having the capability to be able to stick through a class like that for four years.

He nodded his head and gave me a cheeky smile. "Yep! Helps

Miss Willis had great tits and the humor to go with it."

There it was. That sounded more like him.

"Of course, she did…" I muttered, shaking my head. "What are you making anyway?"

"I've got potatoes in the oven, some veggies in this pot, and those, obviously, are New York steaks." He scrunched his face when he stated, "I'd prefer a grill, but I've made do with what we got."

"If they taste as great as they smell, I might not be able to control giving your culinary secret away," I teased and stepped towards him, wrapping an arm around his waist.

"Just as long as others stay private," he smiled shyly and kissed me deeply, "I may be able to forgive your loose tongue." The man pulled away and busied himself with the stove and oven as he told me, "Go and have a seat. I was just about to plate everything before you got here."

True to his word, he plated and served in mere moments after I sat down. He even poured me a glass of wine from a bottle he opened with fragrant flare. The meal was as delicious as our conversation was casual. The atmosphere around us was loose and unhinged from the usual worries of being alone for the first time. It was nice being alone with just each other as company outside the setting we had met in. Near the end of our meal, Brad redirected the conversation.

"I'm glad we decided to do this... even if I won't be able to buy crap food for a while."

"Hey now, I'm having to give up three months of buying coffee," I jested, and we both laughed. "Me too. I've been looking forward to this."

Brad cocked an eyebrow. "Have you now?"

"Course..." I eyed him. "Haven't you?"

A devilish smile came to his lips as he admitted, "More fantasizing than anything."

"Anything in... particular?"

His eyes locked with mine as he said, "Well, it usually starts with you on your knees..."

"...and...?" I knew where it was going, I just wanted to hear him say it.

The man took a breath and held a smile as he said, "Crawling up to me."

"Like this?" I questioned, getting on my knees and crawling under the table. Brad scooted back so I could come up in front of him. "What happens next?"

Brad bit his lower lip. "You pull out my cock."

I fumbled with the buttons of his pants and pulled them down, his cock flopping out from behind his underwear. He was nearly at full length already. I looked up at him like I expected him to know what I was going to ask next.

"Suck," he ordered.

The head of his cock passed my lips without hesitation. I could taste the precum already coming from his tip, the salty tang spreading across my tongue. Brad used a hand to tilt my head up making me look him in the eye with him in my mouth. I covered as much ground as it could as I licked straight up the underside of his cock, earning more precum to pearl out from his head, as he slid slowly in and out.

Our eyes locked yet again and Brad smiled down at me while I worked his swollen head and his hands rested on my cheeks lightly. Spit was running down my chin as he and I both bobbed my head on the upper part of his shaft. He really enjoyed blow jobs, especially the wet and sloppy kind.

A hand of his soon fisted my hair then moved the other to use it to point his cock towards my face when I came up for air. I moved with his motion to capture his cock in my mouth, letting it slide down as far as he wanted and back up to repeat again and again. When Brad let go of my hair, I eagerly sucked on his cock, playing with his head, then moved on to fondle his heavy balls. Soon enough, I found myself sucking on them before switching to gently tugging and his lips formed an "O," but he nodded his head in pleasure.

When my lips returned and recaptured his length once more, Brad grabbed hold of my head again and thrust himself in and out of my mouth. His actions caused his hips to come off the seat he was in while in the act. The force of his face fucking had me coughing several times before actually repelling from him. Coming off his length, I caught my breath before glancing up at him, noticing he wasn't apologetic as he moved a hand behind my head and crashed our lips together into a passionate kiss of tongue and teeth.

Brad broke our duel and stared at my kiss drunk face before declaring, "I'm still going to make you cum first."

"Not if you cum in my ass first," I teased in a snicker.

He gave me a smile then our lips returned to one another's as we both stood up on his side of the table. Brad pushed me away, causing me to fumble towards the bed that dominated the rest of the room then fall onto my back on it. Bouncing on the mattress, he clawed at the rim of my pants after he dove between my legs. My underwear went along with my jeans and were tossed onto the floor in a bundle with haste at the same time as I felt a wet warmth surround my member. Instinctively, I laid a hand on his head while my other rested on the hand he used to trail my stomach and chest, toying with my nipples under my shirt as he made a full sucking motion from my base to tip.

Brad let me pop out of his mouth and stared at me. Driven by desire to take what he wanted, he practically threw my legs into my face and his tongue plunged into my ass with a hunger I hadn't felt from him before. After he unburied himself, I could feel his fingers slowly adding to themselves to loosened me up. When he stuck three fingers in my ass, his mouth was around me again so I couldn't help but shiver beneath him. A whine caught in my throat in the moment he stopped to switch up his tactic by eating me out while jacking me off. The combo was stimulating, and he knew it by the way I arched my back.

"Tell me what you want," the man commanded, a snap of a lid sounding before cool, lubricated fingers prodded at my entrance.

"I want you inside in me..."

"What do you want?" he asked, lining himself up to me and barely pressing his head against my hole.

"Fuck me," I whimpered.

Finally pushing inside, I gripped his arms as he worked his length into me thrust by thrust. "What do you want?" he repeated with a more mischievous tone.

"I want you to fuck me!"

He didn't question me again and plowed me into the bed instead. My legs were around his shoulders while he held onto my hips, which allowed him to keep a ferocious speed. His lips seized mine, making me moan into his mouth before pulling back and pushing my legs down to pin me down. Brad continued his assault on me and fucked me like a whore, and I enjoyed every minute of it as his dick hit my spot that caused me to squirm underneath his strength just right.

Brad allowed my legs to fall wrapping around his waist. He pulled himself close to me wrapping an arm supporting him and a hand to my head. His pace didn't faulter as I rocked beneath him. The palm of his hand rested delicately on my cheek. Before moving to grip the top of my head. Our eyes met and we admired each other's pleasure. The smile on his face was matched by my own.

I raised my head and our smiles met. We locked our lips as if trying not to let the other go. His pace slowed as our kiss became more passionate. While our tongues danced between kisses, Brad maintained a steady thrust into my ass. Going from full speed to a stable pace had me begging for more. Brad could tell by the way I clawed at him to keep him close.

He buried his face in my neck as he breathed, "Fuck…Damon."

"Brad," His name came out of mouth without me thinking.

Pulling back from me he put arms under my shoulders and shifted us up farther on the bed. His cock bumped inside me as he moved about making sure he didn't fall out. Once Brad had me us where he wanted, he put my arms around his neck and rocked me upwards. He had me sitting in his lap still firmly seated on his cock. I curled my legs in around his waist keeping my balance. His hands slid down my back and gave some support as he drew me in close for another kiss. As our lips danced, we rocked our hips against one another. I could tell he was smiling by the way his lips were pressed against mine. The way he moaned into my lips told me just how great my ass felt springing on his cock.

Brad flipped me over in a sudden movement. One moment my arms were wrapped around him and situated in his lap. The next I was on my chest with my ass in the air. He was quick to force himself back inside me. A hand gripped the back of my head and used it as leverage to slam his cock harder into me, hitting the right spot each time as I bounced off his cock with wet slaps that echoed in the small room. The only thing as loud as that were the moans and grunts coming from my mouth.

"Ugh, that's the spot!" I grunted forcing myself back on him.

Brad sniggered at me and pulled my hair harder. He knew I liked being dominated doggy style and it would seem he was intent on winning the bet. With his cock alone, he was bringing me to my climax, but I couldn't let him win just yet. Just as he knew my favorite position, I knew his.

I used the momentum Brad created and caused him to lose his balance. I straddled him, facing away from him. His cock found my hole in a quick movement, and I pinned my legs to his sides. The man felt like he was resisting for a moment before he gave in. Leaning back, I rocked my hips against him. Brad's hands found my hips and he gripped them tightly.

His tone was rough as he said, "Fuck yeah, get it baby."

I felt encouraged to exacerbate myself by working his cock with vigor. My hands supported me from behind while my ass assaulted Brad's cock. I felt his hands slide up my sides and tease my nipples. He rubbed and tugged at them earning whines from me. His hands clasped down on my front, and he brought my back to his chest.

My legs slipped forward and arched along his knees. Brad wrapped his arms around me while using my body weight to keep himself inside. He wrapped an arm around my head and brought me towards him. I could hear him breathing raggedly into my ear. He bit and nipped at my neck as I held onto his arms. Turning my neck as far as I could, our lips met in a sloppy exchange.

Rolling off him, I straddled him once more wanting to be face to face again. Brad made sure his cock found its way back home. Instead of jumping right into another onslaught of stamina, he bucked his hips and held my hips down. He spread my cheeks allowing himself to sink deep inside of me. I felt the tip of his cock pushing the boundary of my own capacity. While he held me there, I swear he was flexing his cock in there. The dirty look on his face only confirmed it.

My hands gripped his sides while the limits of my hole were stretch to no end. I could barely stand the small pumps he gave. Our eyes didn't break their gaze. The smile on his face was so cocky I couldn't help but smile back at him. He spread my cheeks and picked up his pace. I held myself up with my back arched so he had access. My body writhed above him as he kept me locked in his hold. I was enjoying it so much I didn't want it to end.

When he grabbed onto my cock, I knew he was seeking the win. The friction of his hand on my length while his was in my ass was overwhelming. I didn't know how much longer I could hold myself back. It was hard enough to think of anything but cumming at that point.

My mouth crashed against his in a heated exchange of lips and tongue. I pressed so close to him his hand went from my cock to either side of my hips. It took only several more thrusts for both of us to cry out together. Brad's cock pulsed in my ass releasing his seed within me. My own cock exploded hitting him from chest to chin. Our climaxes didn't stop the fun as Brad continued to fuck my hole. I felt his tremors beneath me as he gave multiple rough pumps into me.

I rode out my climax as Brad buried his seed as far as he could as he always liked to. By the end of it, I was twitching and shacking after my body fell to his side. We were both panting like dogs trying to recover. I rolled over only to be received with firm kisses. Brad kissed me as deep as his tongue could go for a moment that lasted longer than it could have been.

Pulling back and through heavy breaths, Brad said, "I... won."

I couldn't help but give an airy laugh. "My ass would say otherwise."

He smiled cheekily and laid a firm hand on my ass, "Two out of three then?"

I gave an unmanly squeal as he attacked me again, already vying for another round.

I just knew this thing, or tryst we had going on... I never wanted it to end.

The end

SKINNY DIPPING

Straight to gay

Kyle Rayne

I need sex tonight. It's time for me to have a rebound fling with a random stranger. I think it'll help me get over my ex. It'll erase her from my mind. I just want straight up dirty stranger fucking.

Everything I own looks like I let my ex-girlfriend pick out all my clothes. I can't find an outfit that says, 'single guy ready to fuck.' Fuck, oh well, I'll have to make do with this. Because jeans aren't as casual as slacks, I wore a button-down shirt and jeans. I'm a stupid ass, but whatever.

As I walked into the bar, I noticed how crowded it was. It was dark with the exception of multicolored lights flashing into the darkness, and there was loud music playing overhead. Something unusual about tonight struck me as my eyes adjusted to the dim lighting... drag queens.

Just to be clear, I'm not prejudiced. It's just that I didn't know there was an event tonight.

As one of them approached me, they were covered in makeup and wearing a sparkly outfit. When they said, "Let me buy you a drink," Lady Gaga was blaring overhead and I could barely hear them.

After nervously running my hands through my hair, I replied, "No thanks, I was just leaving." I received a pouty look and they left.

My way to the exit was blocked by the crowd as it thickened. Several people invited me to dance and offered me drinks. All I could say was, "no thanks." It was such a bad idea, I shouldn't have bothered coming. What did I think? Well, I thought I'd get some pussy...

"Zack!"

As I turned around, I saw someone directly behind me shouting my name. He was an old acquaintance from way back when. He wasn't wearing a drag costume. The only thing he wore was jeans and a t-shirt.

Despite the loud music, I shouted, "Oh, hey Jay. For the record, I didn't know about the special event."

He laughed hysterically, and said, "You didn't know? Do you live under a rock?"

I felt defensive after hearing that. "No! My girlfriend and I just broke up. I'm out of the loop."

While sipping his drink, he said, "Tonight is LGBTQ night, and now you're in the loop."

Oh shit... He was probably bi-sexual or gay. "Well, that's good to know. I'll look elsewhere for my rebound fling."

I could tell he was questioning my sexuality by the way he looked at me. I saw him looking for answers in my eyes.

"I'm straight, so now you're in the loop," I mocked.

As he slowly drew out the words, he said, "Uh huh, alright. I'll give you my number in case you decide to change your mind. I'm gay, and now you're in the loop."

Although I didn't want his number, I took it anyway.

Days passed and I couldn't stop thinking about Jay. There was no doubt he was interested in men, and in me specifically. I guess that's why he gave me his number. It might be a good idea to see Jay for a rebound fling. Actually, it was a terrible fucking idea. In the past, I had never thought about a man sexually, but now I find myself intrigued.

I actually texted Jay after getting some nerve.

"Hey, it's Zack. What are you doing tonight?"

"You apparently. You're looking to fulfill your rebound fling? :-)"

Holy fuck, he was so forthright. I didn't respond because I was embarrassed. After about twenty minutes, he texted me.

"If you're not ready to experiment with a man, we can just chill. I was only kidding anyway."

"Okay."

Now I'm knocking on his door. My palms are sweating nervously. What am I doing here? Do I want to chill or have sex? I don't fucking know anymore…

"Come in," he purred as he waved me in.

At first, I thought I might panic and ask myself, 'what am I doing?'

I felt fine! In fact, I felt better than fine.

Jay walked into the kitchen and said, "Let me show you around."

After that, he gave me a tour of his house, which was very nice.

"Here's the back door, come on, I'll show you my pool."

We walked into his large backyard. There was a sparkling blue pool in the middle, which looked incredibly inviting. Next thing I knew, Jay was stripping naked. I could only see him from behind. He had some ink and a nice fucking body. There's no denying that fucking that body would be nice…

He ran bare-assed to his pool, jumped, and cannon balled into the water like a kid. When he jumped in, I swear I saw his balls poking out from between his thighs. Fuck, I wanted to see them again.

After his epic splash, he came to the surface.

"If you told me you had a pool, I could have brought my trunks."

He laughed and said, "I never wear trunks. Did you see any tan lines on my body? I don't own any, or I'd loan you a pair. "

"Damn, I guess I didn't notice any tan lines. Not that I was looking!"

"I'm not trying to seduce you." Swimming to the other end of the pool, he said, "I would never touch you. You are welcome to leave if you are uncomfortable.

I was surprised at how respectful he was. What did I think? Either he'd shove me in the pool or splash me like a kid. He didn't do either of those to me. I was glad he didn't because my wallet's in my pocket, and I just bought a new phone.

I saw him at the other end of the pool with his back to me. In the shimmering water, I could only see his ass. Although it was blurry, I could see it.

As I watched, I felt myself wanting to see more. When he pulled himself out of the pool and walked to an outdoor kitchen, I was transfixed by his ass. Behind a counter, he opened a refrigerator. He was behind the counter, so I didn't see his dick. I wanted to see his dick now... and his balls, if I'm being honest.

While popping off the top of his cold, frosty bottle, he shouted, "Want a beer?"

"Yeah, I suppose."

From the opposite side of the counter, I picked up the beer after walking around the pool. Sitting on a bar stool, I knew a naked man was only a few feet away. I didn't want to be pervy about it. I've heard of nudist resorts.

My beer was cold, so I took a sip and said, "This is a nice place you have here."

"Thanks, I worked hard and earned it all. I didn't have a rich uncle that died, in case you were wondering."

"It's been so many years since I've seen you. What do you do now?"

"I sell shit on Amazon."

I laughed, "Well, maybe I bought your shit."

"I'm going to the pool again. It's a beautiful day outside. I thought you might like to close your eyes."

After drinking my beer quickly, I felt tipsy. Then I closed my eyes and said, "Damn, and here I thought you'd dance on your counter for me."

In a joking tone, he said, "Well, I wouldn't do it for free."

When I heard him jump in the pool, I knew it was safe to open my eyes. It was so bright that the sun reflected off the water, blinding my eyes. It wasn't possible for me to see him naked. My courage suddenly grew. He wasn't overtly sexual or perverted with his nudity. The man was just comfortable in his own skin. I felt comfortable with him.

Behind the counter, I stripped off my shirt and pants. My nudity was not even mentioned by Jay as he casually swam around his pool.

Jay said, "I will face away from you, so you can get into the pool privately."

In the shallow end, I walked down the steps. It felt so good to cool off in the water on a hot day.

My curiosity was piqued by Jay because he was unlike anything I expected. My first reaction was to think he'd cram his tongue down my throat. Or back float to show off his dick... I wish he did.

At the edge, he rested his elbows on the ledge.

"You're a nice person, for a g-" I cut myself off. The mere suggestion that he would try to hit on me made me feel like an ass. He laughed and I felt relieved that I hadn't offended him.

"I'm gay, not a slutty whore you dick."

I was speechless and a dick.

"What I mean is that I don't hit on straights. I find it really un-fucking cool. I have friends who are straight."

"Of course you have platonic, straight friends. Sorry man."

He shrugged nonchalantly and said, "It's cool, but I need another beer. Want one?"

"Yes, please."

Without warning, he pulled himself out of the pool, but at an angle so I couldn't see his dick. The only thing I saw was his ass. Would I like to see his cock? Yes... yes I did. I wanted more than just a look at it.

I walked to the counter so he wouldn't have to bring me my beer. We were both naked this time, with just the counter separating us.

He was drinking his beer casually and I was glad he couldn't see my dick because it was getting hard. The blood was trickling it up, giving me a semi.

There was something about his body that made me hard... He had firm, tatted pecs. My eyes were drawn to his hips because of his rippling abs. Even his carved V-shaped hips screamed 'sex!'

Aw, fuck, I had a full boner. I wondered if he was hard for me, but I'm a straight man who doesn't think these things... Fuck that. I wasn't a straight man.

Until Jay snapped his fingers in front of me, I had no idea he was talking to me.

"Earth to Zack. Are you alright?"

"Yes, I'm perfect." I bet his dick was perfect.

"You didn't answer my question. How is your sister? Still working at the gas-station?"

It was now or never. I wanted him… I wanted him so bad. Deep down, I know that's why I came here.

"My sister is good. She's an accountant now. Can I suck your dick?"

He spit his beer all over my chest. "I thought you were perfectly straight," he said, looking like a deer caught in headlights.

"Nope. As of now, I'm not."

He cocked an eyebrow and asked, "Is that why you came here?"

"Yes… No, but since I'm here, I'll partake."

"Damn, I told you I wasn't a man whore," he said, rubbing his bare chest. "I've got feelings, you know. You're just gonna use me for my body?"

God, I was such a dick.

"No, I won't use you. It's not like that."

"So, I'm a straight-boy experiment then?" he asked, his voice raspy and deep.

"You're making me feel like a dick. You know what? I've screwed this whole thing up." I picked up my boxers off the bar stool. "There's a reason I'm single."

"Wait, it's alright. Please don't go. We're two consenting adults, yes?"

"Yes, so can I suck your dick now?"

He raked his hands through his hair and said, "Fuck, alright."

"Lie flat on your back," I said as I pointed to his pool raft next to the counter.

Slowly, he stepped out from behind the counter. Finally, I saw his cock! Just thinking about sucking it made my mouth water. He had a thick dick... so thick. The tip was flushed red and his shaft was corded with sinewy veins. There was a line of manscaped fur at the base of his dick.

"Oh my God," I rasped, "You're so fucking big."

His cheeks turned red. "Thanks."

He had a thicker, girthier dick, while I had a longer one. As for my cock, I hoped he'd be equally as impressed. Seeing his eyes fixed on my junk made me feel self-conscious.

"Since you're an expert on good-looking dicks, I hope you like what you see."

"I'm going to ignore your snide comment since your cock looks good. Yep, it passed the dick-inspection."

Laying on the blown-up raft, his dick jutted straight up. My mouth watered at the thought of devouring him. I dropped to my knees in front of the raft. Because of the way he was posed, he looked like a Greek god. He had his hands under his head and his legs splayed out. Fuck, it was seductive as hell.

"You don't have to do this," he rasped.

"I want to... please."

Taking advantage of his open legs, I scooted in between them and pushed his knees apart wider... even wider than they were already.

"Okay, but only if you're sure. Stop if you don't like it. There's no pressure to get me off."

As I fisted his cock, I swallowed his head whole. Oh fuck, this was the sexiest thing I've ever done. His slit was dripping precum into my mouth, and damn, he was tasty. I had no idea I would enjoy sucking dick so much...

I hungrily slid my mouth up and down his length. I was

moaning on his shaft, because I was loving this so much…

His fingers slipped gingerly through my hair until they touched the back of my skull. As he thrust his hips up and down, he pumped his dick into my mouth.

And fuck… it was erotic, naughty and hot.

"You don't have to swallow. F-fuck, you're going to make me cum," he rasped.

My dick was hard… so hard. I spit his dick out with an audible pop.

"Why did you stop? You don't like it?"

"Oh, no that's not it, I like it. It's just… I want to fuck you. Can I still fuck you if you cum in my mouth? Is that a stupid fucking question?"

"It's not stupid. I want you to fuck me, and I'll come with my hand, ok?"

"Okay."

He went to his room to get lube and a condom. Although we could have fucked in his bed, this was cool. It would be my first time fucking in the open without walls.

"Can the neighbors see us?" I asked while rolling the condom down my shaft.

"No, they can't see us. They might be able to hear us, but they aren't home."

"Cool, because I'm not sure that I have a voyeurism-kink."

"Shut up and fuck me."

My dick was rubber-coated and lubricated. After I flipped his legs on my shoulders, his body squeaked on the raft. Seeing his tight puckering hole, I aligned my head at his pink flesh. Pushing into him, fuck... he was tight.

As he moaned, it almost sounded as though he was in pain.

"Hey, are you ok?" I asked.

"I haven't had sex in a while, and I didn't prepare."

"I don't know what that means."

I felt like a dick because I was missing something important...

"I didn't stretch beforehand, but it's fine. I want your dick. Slide in slowly, I'll be okay."

"Alright."

I pressed my dick into his tight flesh. I fucking loved watching his hole swallow up my shaft. He threw his head back and scrunched his eyes shut tight and moaned, "Oh fuck... that feels so good. You can fuck me now. Go slow." It was so hot watching him throw his head back.

My dick glided slowly in and out of his ass, loving how his insides felt so different from pussy's. There was almost a difference in texture between his inner walls and a cunt's.

He was being fucked hard, slow, and deep by me. It was a balls-deep slide every time. It was not enough for me. Leaning forward, I kissed him.

While moaning, I flicked my tongue around in his mouth. It was the best sex of my life, and I wanted more. My heart never wanted this to end, even though I knew it would eventually come to an end. I was going to cum soon.

"Fuck me faster," he rasped as he pulled away from our kiss.

I was fucking him like an animal in no time. The inflatable raft squeaked incessantly under our bodies. Moreover, I was moaning so loudly that I think the whole block could hear me. I didn't give a damn. I hadn't been laid in so long.

I had this muscle-clad man under me moaning and squealing with his eyes shut tight. I was fucking him so hard and so fast that his dick was bouncing from side to side on his hard body. While fucking him, I was going to jerk him off. As I pounded into his ass, I fisted his cock. Since my hand was dry, I spit on it and started jerking him off again, faster this time.

"Oh fucking fuck!" he cried.

I must be doing something right.

"That's it," I rasped.

"I'm going to cum!" he shouted.

As soon as I grabbed the base of the condom, I pulled my dick out. My mouth watered when I thought about tasting him. There was no way I wasn't going to drink him and swallow every drop.

When I sucked his head into my mouth, he started pumping his load.

"Oh fuck!" he moaned and grabbed fistfuls of my hair. My scalp tingled with pleasure as he pulled my hair.

In a delicious way, his juices were slightly salty and tangy. What chick wouldn't want to swallow? I always found gagging such a buzz-kill on my after-sex endorphin high. But me? I sucked every last drop out of him.

"Okay," he rasped and pulled his dick outta my mouth. "Did you cum yet?" he asked.

"No, I wanted to swallow you."

"You can cum in my ass or mouth."

"Fuck, that's a hard choice."

Since there was so much I wanted to try, I hoped this wasn't a one-time thing.

"I want to cum in your mouth," I said and took the condom off. "Are you sure the rubber taste won't bother you?"

Not that I've sucked dick before, I just know from past women who sucked me off after I fucked them.

"Are you kidding me? I fucking love it for some weird reason. Now, lay down on the raft."

It felt so fucking good to be sucked into his mouth. Watching a man suck my dick was better than anything I've experienced. It was so fucking hot! In a way I couldn't describe, it was so naughty and sexy.

I watched him suck up and down my length with rapt attention. He stroked my shaft with his hand and sucked me at the same time! I hadn't thought to do that... I was still so new to this.

My hips jerked when I felt a finger press into my hole. He spit my dick out and asked, "Should I stop?"

"Keep going, finger my ass." I grabbed the lube and squirted it all over his hand.

"Damn that's a lot of lube."

"Hopefully you'll use lots of fingers."

When I said that, he sucked my dick back into his mouth. His finger was so well-oiled that it glided right in. It was such a new sensation for me. There was a burning, tingling sensation to it.

"Another finger."

He pressed another one inside... then another. Next time, I want his dick. For now, his fingers will do. I wasn't sure how many were inside of me. Two, or three? Fuck, maybe four.

My crown was sucked with intense pressure, pushing me over the edge. The cum was flowing deep into his mouth as I spurted it.

"Oh God. Oh fuck, I'm coming!" I moaned. It was the most intense orgasm of my life. Next time, I'd get him to fuck me in the ass.

It started out as a rebound relationship, but ended up becoming so much more. We became partners and lovers. He was my best friend.

It turns out I love getting fucked in the ass.

"Please... please fuck me tonight," I begged while he was working on his computer.

"Whatever you want, my sexy power-bottom."

He was going to be busy for the next hour or so. So, I got my favorite dildo to stretch myself out.

"Get on the bed for me," he rasped.

"Fuck, alright. I've only been waiting for an hour!"

When he came to bed, he fucked me deep, hard and fast. My legs were over his shoulders, and my feet were up in the air. That's the way I loved it! He thrust in and out of me while I jerked my dick. I wasn't going to last long...

The next thing I knew, I was shooting my load all over my stomach. I was wet, sticky and satisfied.

"I'm coming so hard!" he moaned while shooting his load deep... so deep inside me.

The end

Dear reader... Thanks for reding! Enjoy a free book!

All of my bookd are here

TWINK

Straight to gay

Kyle Rayne

H

ere I am at a bachelor party, although I am not the one getting married. The groom's party is at his house while his bride's party is elsewhere.

As we wait for the strippers to arrive, we're all taking shots of tequila. Just one shot, salt and lime wedge included, and that's all I need!

As the music blared so loudly, we almost missed the knock on the door. Strippers flooded into the house as the bachelor John opened the door. There were male and female strippers among them, some of whom were dressed in costumes.

"Hey John, did you notice some of your strippers are dudes?" I awkwardly asked.

"Yeah, I was the one who paid for them. Every stripper was hand-picked by me. My gay friends don't want to stare at tits all night, so don't be a dick."

Suddenly, I felt defensive and said, "I understand and I'm not being a dick."

I got a sucker punch from John and he said, "Well, it's tits for you. Keep your eyes off the men if you don't like what you see." Then he chased a few women down a hallway into a bedroom. They were laughing and giggling as the bedroom door closed behind them.

Male strippers were already shirtless and I couldn't stop staring at their bodies. It was amazing how well-muscled and strong their arms were. All of them had rippling ads and hips carved into a V that disappeared into skimpy shorts. Although I was in decent shape, I wasn't like that. Still, I considered myself attractive.

As a gay man, I couldn't help but stare at the sexy men. There were a few people who knew, but I hadn't come out to my family yet. It was for a good reason that I never posted pictures of myself and my past partners on social media. I was always accused of being secretive by my family. The correct word was private, in my defense.

People were dancing to the loud music. The strippers performed for the guests while they sat on the couches. Male entertainers included...

In the kitchen, some of the male entertainers were helping themselves to liquor, and I noticed one guy in particular.

Oh fuck, he was a cutie. His hair was blonde and his eyes were dark green. He had a nice body with natural muscles. Rather than bloated like a beefcake, he looked lean. When I looked at him from behind, I had fantasies about all the things I would do to his ass. Because he was smaller than me, I wanted to wreck him in my bed. With his legs slung over my shoulders, I knew his feet would look good up in the air.

I was intrigued by his innocent boyish look. There was just something about him that didn't feel like he wasn't right for this gig. There was a story, and I wanted to hear it all.

God, I couldn't believe how fucking adorable he was. He wasn't even drinking beer or tequila. Of all things, he was talking to someone while drinking a fucking Sprite. He definitely had a magnetic personality. Three people were trying to get his attention, two of them female coworkers. I had to get him away from them so I could have him all to myself.

After I shoved my way into their little circle, directly behind him, I said, "Ladies, we need you in the living room. It's the boss's order or you won't be paid."

They scampered out of the kitchen like cockroaches.

As I stood behind him, I could smell his hair, and I tried not to lean forward and sniff him. After taking a deep breath, I inhaled his scent. Fuck, he smelt so good... He only wore little black briefs and I was directly behind his ass when he turned around and said, "Oh hey." His cheeks were flushed red and he didn't seem to be used to his job.

"First night on the job?"

Nervously, he ran his hands through his hair and said, "Yeah, it's that obvious, isn't it?" He had a deep, husky voice that cracked with nervousness.

"Yes, it is," I said, and I noticed he was now sandwiched between me and some other guy I didn't recognize. I didn't want a threesome tonight because I wanted him all to myself. Wait, fuck, I'm not trying to seduce the help. I'll help him get away from prying eyes.

I could see the other guy glowering at me. Obviously, he was thinking the same thing as I was. However, I would win this game and get this little stripper's attention.

I shoved a few beer bottles into his hands and ushered him out of the kitchen. I said loud enough for the other guy to hear, "John wants you to serve drinks."
"What should I do with the beers?" he asked as we entered an empty living room. "Everyone left, where did they go?"
"They are all in the bedrooms," I replied, taking the beers from him and setting them down on the coffee table. "You don't have to serve drinks. I was just giving you an out. As far as I can tell, you do not enjoy walking around looking *like that*." I waved a finger up and down his body.
His cheeks blushed an even deeper shade of red and he asked, "What do I look like?"
After nearly choking on my beer, I cautiously said, "You look like fucking sex on a stick, ready to be devoured."

Poor guy was speechless. As I sat down on the couch, his crotch was nearly at eye level. I was not old, but he was younger than me. I'd love to turn him into my twink... And I want him to dance for me. Although it was his job tonight, I felt bad sexualizing him.

Instead, I threw him my jacket and said, "Tie it around your waist or wear it."
"Thanks."

He put on the jacket and sat down next to me. I might be able to get him to dance for me if I am nice to him.
"So, why did you take this job?"
He picked up a beer and said, "Well, for money obviously."
I laughed so hard and said, "Why didn't you go work at the grocery store?"
His face was so red, even his ears were starting to blush. "I was told I could earn cash tips."
"You can get tips from serving tables."

It made me feel bad for him that he didn't say anything. He deserved a successful first night, at least he could make some money.
"Dance for me. I'll tip you."

I knew immediately from his intimidated gaze that he was straight when he locked eyes with mine.
"I swear I won't bite. After your shift, I'll take you out to dinner if you're a good dancer."
"You know what?" he crassly said, "I quit."

Fuck, I felt like such a dick. I could tell he didn't like being sexually objectified. As he got up, he threw my jacket at me.

As he headed towards the door, I called out, "Wait, I'll still take you to dinner. You don't need to dance for me."
He looked at me wide eyed and asked, "Why are you being so nice to me?"
I didn't really know, but I said, "So I can get to know you better. Here's my number, and the offer for dinner is still on the table."

I wanted to have sex with him and it was a long shot, but it didn't mean I wouldn't try. As soon as I walked him outside to his car, I made sure he had my number entered correctly in his phone, and after that, he was gone.

Whoa, what the fuck did I do? I scared the shit out of a young straight man and made him quit his job. You know what though? He was too good for a gig like this. He was too cute, innocent and naive. I didn't even know *his* name, because he didn't tell me.

Now that he was gone, I went inside to enjoy the rest of my night. He wasn't anything like these experienced male entertainers who were giving me lap dances. These strippers were very good at their job. I'd be out of cash in no time.

I kept shoving my hard earned cash down their little tight briefs. There was no doubt I loved me some dick, and for the most part, I could see their dick-prints through the thin fabric. There were some guys, however, who were stuffing their bulge with socks, or something.

Fuck, I couldn't take it anymore, these guys were giving me a boner. A dancer grinded his ass against my crotch. He did this on purpose. As far as I understood, we weren't supposed to touch them. I didn't hesitate to spank him. My hands smacked each ass cheek and I said, "Okay big boy, that's enough. I need to go home now."
I really needed to go home and clear the pipes.
After a week, I actually heard from the cute ex-stripper, Danny. We were eating at a franchise breakfast joint, and I couldn't believe he asked me here. He told me about his school and new job. He tried the stripping gig to help pay for college, he explained. But he never went back after the night we met.

It wasn't clear to me if it was a date or just a platonic thing. Usually I can tell right away, but I couldn't figure it out.
The entire time I kept saying to myself, *"Don't fuck this up. Don't push him, he'll freak out."*

This time when I walked him to his car I said, "You want to go back to my place?"

He fumbled with his keys, and said, "Sure, I'll follow you there."

As I took him back to my apartment, I didn't know what I was going to do. Should I try to romance him to get him to bed? Fuck, I didn't know. Maybe I'll just kiss him and see what happens. I hated coming across as *that* gay guy, but whatever.

"Welcome to my apartment."

I felt so damn awkward. What were we supposed to do if we weren't going to do something intimate? I wasn't sure if he just wanted a friend… or something more.

I attempted to be a normal human being and dragged my mind out of the gutter and asked, "Want to watch a sci-fi movie on Netflix?"

"Yeah, sure."

He sat down near me on the couch, our thighs touching, and he didn't move. In an effort to be polite, I put the movie on.

"This is my favorite movie."

Just like when I met him the first time, Danny's cheeks were flushing red.

"Am I making you uncomfortable?" I asked. Our thighs were still touching.

"No. I… Can I kiss you?" he shyly asked.

I leaned forward and kissed him on the cheek.

"Yes, if that's what you want."

If I was lucky, he'd let me suck his dick or lick his ass. But kissing is good, I'd take the kiss.

I sucked his bottom lip into my mouth and he groaned. Then I playfully sucked on his earlobe. His voice was deep and raspy when he said, "Damn, you are skilled with your mouth."

I whispered in his ear, "You have no idea." I licked down his neck and said, "I can do lots of fun things with my mouth." I loved giving oral sex, it was my favorite.

His arms broke out in gooseflesh and I licked the seam of his lips until he opened his mouth. He wrapped his arms around my neck and I devoured him. I couldn't help but to kiss him so aggressively and fuck… my dick was so damn hard. My boner was pressing against my jeans at an odd angle and I had to adjust myself.

Although it's not polite to kiss with your eyes open, I looked to see if he was hard for me… he was.

My hands slid down his chest and stomach, remembering

how sinewy his body was. I couldn't believe he was actually letting me touch him. Can you remember what it's like to touch someone before you've had sex? There's something incredibly intoxicating about it.

I poked a finger inside his pants and teased his hips. His skin was so fucking soft.

"Tell me what you want," I rasped. "I don't want to do anything you're not ready for. We'll take it one day at a time." Oh, yes I was suggesting this wasn't a one-time thing. I'd keep taking him to my bed as long as he let me, and that thought reminded me. "My bed is more comfortable than the couch."

"Bed, yes," he mumbled.

Yes! I couldn't believe I was showing him to my bedroom. I got on my bed and got comfortable.

"Let's just kiss and cuddle," I said to make him feel comfortable. "If you want more, I'll give you anything you want. But you can leave whenever you want."

"Oh… Okay."

The moment he got on my bed, I wanted to fuck him, but I could wait. We were kissing again in no time. Getting on top of me, he pinned my wrists over my head as I lay flat on my back.

I pulled away from our kiss. "Damn, that's hot. Have your way with me."

"Yes, yes I will," Danny deeply rasped.

With such ravenous passion, he kissed me into the mattress. His hips were grinding against mine, essentially dry humping me.

My wrists were still pinned down when I pulled away again and said, "This would feel better if we took our pants off. My zipper is chafing my balls."

"Should I get naked?" he shyly asked.

"Only if you want to." *Please say yes.*

After letting go of my wrists, he undressed in a sexy manner that seemed practiced.

"Wow, that's hot. Am I the only one who's got to see your stripper moves?"

He blushed and said, "Yes."

"Can you show me your special dance moves?" I asked.

He was just wearing his sexy tight black boxer briefs.

He deeply laughed and said, "I don't know if they are special. I only practiced in front of a mirror."

"Perfect. Put some music on, whatever you practiced too."

When he started dancing to some music on YouTube, I was instantly hypnotized by the fluidity of his movements. I was transfixed by the dips and curves of his abs, the sharp points of his hips and spine, and by the clavicle that looked so deep.

He straddled my hips and was thrusting his hips right in front of me and his bulge was right in my face.

"Fuck, you're sexy as hell."

I grasped his hips and let them move with the gyrating of his hips.

"You're still dressed. It's your turn to get naked and give me a show," Danny chided.

I laughed and said, "I'll try, but I won't be nearly as sexy and graceful as you."

He ruffled my hair and said, "Let's see what you got."

I started with my shirt, then my pants. As I tried to dance a sexy, Danny laughed at me.

"Ok, enough dancing from me. Need some help with that?" I pointed to his semi erect boner. Fuck, I wanted to see his dick, even if he wouldn't let me touch it.

As he stood up, he slowly pulled his boxers down until his balls and dick popped out and I groaned. I wanted to suck his dick and lick his balls so bad. I wanted to swallow every last drop out of him.

His hard dick swayed from side to side as Danny danced slowly and hypnotically. Since I wasn't sure if it was okay to touch him, I placed my hands on his hips. I was inches away from his dick. Honestly, he was such a fucking tease. Imagine putting a steak in front of a shark.

"Can I suck your dick please?" I asked.

He looked like he was considering it. I was also sure he could feel my breath on his shaft when I said, "You don't have to get me off in return."

"Okay, you can suck me."

I slurped him into my mouth as quickly as I could.

"Oh fuck," he moaned, "Your tongue, your mouth. Oh god."

When I sucked his shaft to his head, I flicked my tongue at the sensitive V on the underside of his head.

He grasped a handful of my hair and moaned, "That feels so good."

"I told you I was skilled with my tongue." I cupped the globes of his ass and slid a hand over his crack. "You've never been licked back there, have you?"

He blushed and said, "No, but if you want too-"
I interrupted him and said, "Yes, I definitely do."

I grabbed his hips and flipped him on all fours, and he made a sound of shock. In the blink of an eye, I opened his cheeks and dove face first into his ass. When I circled my tongue around his hole, he moaned.
While he didn't have much taste, he smelled fresh and clean.
"You cleaned up before," I teased.
"Yes, I was prepared. I've never done this before, but I did it just in case."
So, he did want to have sex with me then.

When I licked my tongue across his ring of muscle, it quivered. My cock wanted to be buried inside him, but I wasn't sure if that would happen today. It didn't matter to me, since I was enjoying rimming him with my tongue. When I pressed my tongue into his ass, he moaned. This time, he really moaned. I pushed my tongue inside him as far as it would go.
"Oh God, that's amazing," he moaned.
"My dick is pretty amazing too. I bet you that would feel even better." I flicked my tongue over his hole.
I stopped and said, "It's ok to tell me what you want, or what you don't want."
He looked at me over his shoulder and said, "I want you... I want you, inside of me."
This was the best day of my life. This cute guy was officially my twink.
"Lay down flat on your back for me baby," I purred.
His cock jutted up in the air as he flipped over on his back.
"I could fuck you doggy style, but I want to see your face," I said while rolling the condom down my shaft.

Then I slipped two lubed fingers into his hole, so I could get some lube inside of him. I did this a few times, actually. His pink hole was wet... so wet and ripe for fucking.

As I climbed in between his legs, I put his knees on the crooks of my elbows. His body looked so good like this—fully ready to be fucked. He was slender and muscular at the same time. Shadows from dim lighting accentuated every curve and dip of his body.
I pressed my head at his entrance and my head slipped in fairly easily. His eyebrows were scrunched as he closed his eyes.
"You okay, baby?" I didn't want to hurt him.

"Oh, it feels so good. Keep going."

Slowly, I pushed myself in. My entire length was pushed inside of him inch by inch. I loved watching his pink hole swallow my entire dick. Now I was balls deep. Danny moaned and dug his fingernails into my hips. I hadn't started thrusting yet. He needed a moment to adjust.

"Oh fuck, your dick... Your dick feels so good."

"That's what I wanted to hear. Can I fuck you now?"

"Yes, please, yes. Fuck me," he begged with a lusty voice.

"Whatever you want, babe."

My dick slid in and outta his ass. I thrust into him pretty hard, and his eyes were tightly shut. He was still grabbing my hips, helping to guide me in and out at an angle that he liked. My shaft may have dragged across his prostate a few times.

Looking down, his dick was hard and leaking precum. His shaft was slick and his crown was glistening with wetness. To get his juices, I jerked his dick while fucking him, then licked it off my hand.

"When you cum, let me know. I'm going to swallow you."

"I can't believe it, I'm already almost there. I'm so fucking close," Danny rasped.

It's selfish, but I wanted to cum first, then finish him with my mouth. I was close too. His ass was so tight and so hot. I could feel the warmth of his body through the rubber. Every time his hole quivered, his insides milked my shaft. Just a little spasm of his channel was all it took for me to start coming, my load filling up the condom.

"Oh fucking... oh Danny," I rasped, still unable to believe this little twink let me nail him

I grabbed the condom base and pulled my dick out, then I sucked him in my mouth. His nuts were red, high and tight. He needed to cum, and he was almost there.

As he thrust into my mouth, he planted his feet firmly into the mattress. My goal was to give him the best blowjob of his life. As his crown bounced off the back of my throat, I tasted ample amounts of precum.

I knew he was there when he grabbed handfuls of my hair.

"Oh fuck, I'm coming... I'm coming so fucking hard!"

His load pumped into my mouth, and I gulped down every last drop.

The end

POWER BOTTOM

Straight to gay

Kyle Rayne